SECRETS

OF THE

REALM

A Novel by
Bev Stout

ISBN: 1484832280
ISBN-13: 978-1484832288

Cover design by W. R. Stout based on a painting *Ship at Sea, Sunset* by Edward Moran (1829-1901)

To my husband, Dick.
He's my rock, my biggest fan.

ACKNOWLEDGEMENTS

Special thanks to Kody for your endless enthusiasm. Kelsey and Emily, two of my earlier readers. Deanna for her gentle push. Vicky and Kathi for being there during the whole process. Thank you Bill, Sydney, Carter, Chrissy, Paul, Sean and Morgan. Mom and Dad. Mike and Margaret, there at the beginning. Mark, for his inspiration to get Secrets in print. Love to all my friends and family, now and always.

CHAPTER ONE

Annie ran her fingers through what was left of her black hair. "You sheared me like a sheep, you did."

"Keep your bloody voice down." Erik motioned toward the thatch-roof cottage. "Don't want to wake her."

Fifteen-year-old Annie shivered at the mere thought of waking Aunt Mary. Annie doubted she could survive another whipping.

For eight years, Aunt Mary blamed Annie for any troubles that happened to their family. She was nothing more than a nuisance, another mouth to feed. But this was worse, far worse. Uncle William was dead, and Aunt Mary blamed Annie for it.

Holding the lantern close to Annie's face, Erik studied the hair he had cut just below her ears. His eyes then shifted to his younger brother's clothing now hanging loosely on Annie's slim frame. "Not much we can do 'bout that," he said with a shrug.

While her cousin brushed the tufts of hair from her shoulders, Annie pulled up on the breeches. "You really think I can pass myself off as a boy?" she asked.

"Never thought you looked much like a girl."

"I beg your pardon," Annie said as she slammed her fist into Erik's stomach.

He grabbed her wrist before she could land another blow. "And you certainly are no lady," he whispered. "But that's good, 'cause on the streets of London, you need to fit in with them other beggars looking for work."

"I can do this," Annie said, trying her best to sound convincing.

"You have no choice."

"Come with me, Erik," Annie said.

He shook his head. "This is the only life I have ever known, taking care of the Spencer's grounds with my... my father."

In the lantern's glow, Annie saw tears welling in Erik's eyes. She took his hand. "He's dead, Erik. There is nothing for you here."

"I know you will never understand, but I can't leave my family, especially now with Father gone. They need me."

Unfortunately, Annie did understand. Aunt Mary was still his mother, and James and Thomas, his brothers. Nothing would change that.

"Promise me you will be careful," she said. "If Aunt Mary learns you helped me, her whip will find your back as well; and please keep Abigail from finding out for as long as you can. I can't risk the Spencer's searching for me."

"If Abigail comes around looking for you, what should I tell her?"

"Tell her I am grieving. That won't be a lie." Annie thought a moment. "When she learns I'm gone, do you think she will cry or just start throwing things?"

"Abigail has quite a temper. I'll be sure to duck," Erik said while he tenderly draped the coat over Annie's shoulders. "I put some biscuits in the pockets for you."

"I will never forget you, Erik" Annie said before hurrying down the moonlit road.

CHAPTER TWO

Two days of begging on the streets of London netted Annie one moldy crust of bread and a swat from a shopkeeper's broom. She didn't fare much better during her nights in a garbage-strewn alley. Bolting upright every time rats invaded her space, she got little sleep.

But it was the drunkards and thieves stumbling through the alley that concerned Annie the most. Hoping she wouldn't be discovered, Annie tried to make herself one with the wall she huddled up against while she listened to their profanity-laced voices.

When light broke through the morning fog, Annie hugged her knees close to her chest. Her stomach began to rumble.

Annie stood up and shoved her hands deep into her pockets finding only remnants of the biscuits Erik had given her. She turned the pockets inside out. Crumbs rained down on the rats scurrying at her feet. "At least you won't go hungry today," she said.

To obliterate the soft lines of her face, she scooped up handfuls of dirt and rubbed it into her forehead and cheeks. Satisfied she could carry off the masquerade, Annie hiked the breeches above her waist and strode out of the alley. She zigzagged her way across the narrow cobblestone street, dodging horse-drawn carts and scavenging dogs.

She had heard word on the street that Captain Hawke needed a new cabin boy. Making her way to the wharf, she wandered past a group of foul smelling and equally foul talking lads who would be vying for the same job as she. Looking at the boys, Annie believed her small size would be more of an asset than a liability.

But Annie's fascination wasn't on the boys or the sailors hauling supplies, it was on the ship moored at the dock. While she gazed up at the Realm, Annie felt someone yank her coat sleeve. "Let go," she said.

The youth yanked even harder. "Make me," he taunted her.

Annie attempted to knee him in the crotch, but he shifted his nimble body out of range. "Did you hear me? Let go my sleeve," she again yelled.

The smaller bully was joined by a larger one who grabbed Annie's other sleeve. They jerked her back and forth in a lopsided game of tug-of-war. When her slender arms bent sharply behind her back, the coat slid off. The boys then tossed their ill-gotten prize into the air.

"Give me back my coat!" she shouted. The coat was more than buttons and wool to Annie. It was Erik's last kindness to her, a final hug.

Distracted by the new game of keep-away, she didn't see yet another boy racing behind her. He rammed the heels of his hands into Annie's shoulder blades knocking her to the ground. "You jump like a bloody girl," he said.

"Girl?" Annie muttered under her breath, "I'll show him *girl*."

Springing to her feet, she ignored the throbbing pain in her back. She whirled around, giving the boy an uppercut to his square jaw before kicking him in the shin. He tumbled to his knees groaning while Annie dashed behind a broad-shouldered teenager who showed little interest in the tomfoolery of his shorter competitors.

Peering out from behind her brawny fortress, Annie yelled at the injured boy as he nursed his sore jaw and aching shin. "You scurvy little vermin, I have come too far to let the likes of you stop me!"

* * *

On the larboard deck of the Realm, Captain Jonathan Hawke surveyed the boys on the wharf. Their antics did not amuse him.

A sailor since the age of thirteen, the captain began his life at sea as a bosun mate in charge of rigging and sails. Ten years later, he was England's most celebrated merchant ship captain.

He had never been a cabin boy and found them to be more of a bother than anything else, but Mr. Montgomery insisted he employ one. To keep his fastidious first mate and best friend happy, Captain Hawke would again hire one.

While the captain observed the boys on the wharf, one ruffian grabbed his attention, the one who had delivered an impressive kick to his assailant's shin.

Mr. Montgomery pointed to the same street urchin the captain was looking at. "What do you think of that one?"

"He's a spirited one. I will give him that. But unless he can gain a few inches in height and girth before we set sail, he shan't be my cabin boy," Captain Hawke said with a chuckle.

* * *

Glancing over each shoulder, Annie prepared for another attack; but the unruly boys had become as still as the stone lions that guarded Lord Spencer's manor home. Annie followed their gaze to the two men marching down the gangway.

"That's 'im—Cap'n 'awke!" one boy shouted in a heavy cockney accent.

Oh my, he is a fine looking bloke, Annie thought. The uncommonly tall gentleman she gawked at wore a well-fitted waistcoat and tan linen breeches. He sported a neatly trimmed mustache, and a ribbon tied back his sandy blond hair.

Annie soon realized it was not the well-dressed man who mesmerized the boys. Their interest was on the other, the one who stood slightly shorter than his shipmate. She smiled to herself. Captain Hawke certainly didn't look like any gentleman she had ever seen before.

Unlike his impeccably groomed first mate, Captain Hawke's tangled black hair fell below a scarf peeking out from beneath a weathered tricorn hat. While a single button fastened his shirt at his trim waist, stained trousers disappeared into black boots that came up to his knees.

Annie mused how seventeen-year-old Abigail would have described the captain as wickedly handsome. Days earlier, she and Abigail had sat on the edge of Abigail's four-poster bed while Annie listened to her friend's favorite subject—men. She wondered what Abigail would think if she knew Annie might be spending her days and nights in the company of men, only men. Scandalous, she thought.

Annie twisted a button on her shirt while she watched several boys doff their caps in respect and eager anticipation. Chosen or not, she knew Captain Hawke's decision would set the course for each of their lives.

With a jaunty bounce to his step, the first mate walked down the gangway. Reaching the wharf, Mr. Montgomery stopped to inspect casks and barrels destined for the American colonies while Captain Hawke consulted with several sailors about the goods secured in the cargo hold.

As the captain and his first mate drew closer, the boys gave them a wide berth. "Form a straight line. Stand at attention," Mr. Montgomery ordered. He motioned to Annie to follow suit. He then took one step back, legs slightly apart and arms behind his back.

While Annie and the others jockeyed for position, she could not help but notice how much bigger the boys were than she was. Ha, she thought, they do not stand a chance of being hired as a cabin boy.

The captain strutted back and forth. He paused in front of the lad wearing Annie's coat. The boy's arms jutted out from its sleeves while split-opened seams accommodated his hefty size. Captain Hawke called to Annie, "Want your coat back, boy?"

Annie looked at the captain out the corner of her eye. While gnawing on her lower lip, she shook her head. "No."

"Suit yourself," he said as he proceeded to look over each boy from head to toe.

One boy rolled up his sleeve, flexing his arm to show off his scrawny muscle. Another displayed hands callused from manual work. When Captain Hawke stopped in front of Annie, she exhibited nothing.

He raised his eyebrow at her. "What is your name, boy, and how old are you?" As intimidating as he looked, Captain Hawke was surprisingly soft spoken.

Annie had expected the captain to inquire about her age. He had asked everyone that question. But he asked the name of only one other youth, the broad-shouldered lad Annie had earlier hidden behind, Lawrence.

She nervously shifted her weight from one foot to the other.

"What's the matter, boy, you gotta piss?"

"No, sir." Annie stopped fidgeting and stood straight. Yes, she decided, her great great grandfather's name would become her name. She remembered the stories told about how he had sailed with the ill-fated

Spanish Armada. In 1588, the fishing village of Staithes, on the rugged North Yorkshire coast of England, became his salvation. In 1726, it became Annie's birthplace.

"My name..."

Captain Hawke stopped her in mid-sentence. "Look at me when you speak."

She gazed up into the dark eyes peering down on her. "My name is Andrés de la Cruz, sir, and I am fourteen years old." She hated lying about her age, but Erik had reminded her often how she didn't look fifteen.

"Fourteen, you say." The captain stepped back and stroked his stubby beard. "You barely look thirteen. The truth now, how old are you?"

"If it pleases you, sir, I am thirteen."

The boys on either side of Annie snickered.

"It neither pleases nor displeases me." He pointed toward the boys. "Have you noticed that these fine chaps are bigger than you are? So, why should I hire one as puny as you and not one of them?"

"I cannot help what I lack in size, sir, but I can assure you that I am a hard worker. You will not be disappointed."

"Good answer." His eyes narrowed as he leaned down and whispered, "You are not fooling me. I am no stranger to deception."

Annie sucked in her breath.

Captain Hawke stared into her ice blue eyes. "You're no Spaniard. You're a well-educated

Englishman."

Air and relief rushed from Annie's lungs.

He ran his knuckle roughly across her cheekbone where the remains of a black eye lingered. "How many fights you been in, boy?"

Annie flinched at his touch. "Not a one, sir. A shopkeeper, the old sot, backhanded me across my face." She reached up and lightly touched below her eye. "London is not kind to her beggars."

The captain laughed before he resumed going down the line of eleven boys. He returned, hesitating in front of Annie.

Confident, she pulled her shoulders back, and prepared for the announcement, but Captain Hawke walked away and approached the tall lad, Lawrence.

"Congratulations," he said.

Annie heard little enthusiasm in Captain Hawke's voice. When she saw the captain about to shake Lawrence's hand, her disappointment boiled over. "Why him and not me?" Annie shrieked. "Look at him. He's too big to be a cabin boy."

Not waiting for the explanation she knew would never come, Annie rushed behind Lawrence. With her head bent low, she ran full force butting him in the curve of his back. The lad's knees buckled. The captain jumped back just in time.

With Lawrence lying face down at the captain's feet, Annie pounced on his back and struck him with her fists. Dazed, Lawrence didn't react until Captain Hawke pried Annie off him.

His nose bloodied and his lip torn, Lawrence leapt to his feet. While Annie struggled in the captain's vice-like grip, the youth threw a punch to the left side of her face. The blow jerked her head sideways. Blood warmed the captain's palm, not from the blood dripping from Annie's mouth, but from the blood seeping through the back of her shirt.

Drawing a square-handled knife from its sheath, Lawrence lunged at Annie. His eyes raged. "I'll gut you like a fish!" he shouted.

The captain propelled Annie out of the way and pulled out his ivory-handled knife. "You don't want to do that, lad," Captain Hawke said, his voice calm, as he danced out of the way of the youth slashing at him through empty air.

"Me money's on the captain," said the boy wearing Annie's coat.

Another youth hollered above the growing crowd, "A shilling says Lawrence draws first blood!"

Annie sprang to her feet. Dazzled by the captain's footwork, she joined in the debate. "Lawrence is outmatched. He won't hit his mark. Besides, the captain has no intention of harming him."

"Are you daft? If the captain gets a chance, he will have Lawrence's gizzards for supper, he will."

Annie couldn't read minds, but she did have a keen sense of observation. She noted the subtle movements of the captain and his first mate—the rise of a chin, a quick glance of an eye, a gesture of the hand. Annie understood it all. Captain Hawke wanted

Mr. Montgomery to intervene, but his first mate carried no weapon. More importantly, he did not wish to dirty his clothes.

The captain gave him no choice. "Take him!"

In a blur of motion, Mr. Montgomery tackled Lawrence, wrestling him to the ground. He slammed the youth's face into the wharf not once, but twice. Grasping Lawrence's wrist, Mr. Montgomery pounded his hand onto the wharf's uneven planks.

"Give it up, boy!" The first mate demanded.

When Lawrence's fingers opened, Mr. Montgomery seized the knife and hurled it off the wharf. It arced in the air before plunging through the water leaving not a ripple.

Lawrence's crumpled body lay in the captain's shadow.

"On your feet!" Captain Hawke ordered.

Lawrence rose amid jeers and laughter from the boys and sailors who witnessed the raucous affair. Twisting Lawrence's arm behind his back, Mr. Montgomery quickly hustled him off the wharf.

Lawrence's humiliation was far worse than his injuries. As bloody spittle ran down his chin, he shouted back at Annie, "I swear to you, Andrés de la Cruz, you will regret this day! When you least expect it, I will slit your throat." He paused. "That is a promise."

The boys moved out of the way as the captain marched toward Annie.

"Are you satisfied?"

"Beggin' your pardon, sir?"

While Annie wiped blood from the corner of her mouth with her sleeve, she stumbled backward, her legs splayed out in front of her.

Looming over Annie, Captain Hawke clenched his fists. "Since you started this nonsense, are you satisfied?"

Annie wished she could coil a strand of hair around her finger, but she had to be content with pulling on the hem of her shirt. "Uh, yes, sir. No one got killed."

Captain Hawke scanned the boys replaying the aborted knife attack. They cheered as one boy spun in a circle before landing flat on his back. With an imaginary dagger clutched to his heart, the boy's body twitched once more.

"They wanted blood—anyone's," Captain Hawke muttered.

Annie scrambled to her feet. "Between you and me, Captain, they are an immature lot. As for that Lawrence fellow, it's those quiet ones you gotta look out for. One moment they are not saying a word and the next, they are a raving lunatic."

"And here I thought *you* were the quiet one," Captain Hawke said. "But instead, you are both amusing and daring."

Annie beamed at the compliment. "Thank you, sir." She almost curtsied before remembering she was now Andrés de la Cruz.

When the captain jabbed her sharply in the

shoulder with his fingers, her grin vanished.

"Let me give you some advice, boy. You are too daring for your own good, and the element of surprise will not always be in your favor." His left eyebrow shot up. "You must earn the respect of your fellow shipmates. Have I made myself clear?"

"Yes, perfectly, sir." Annie swallowed hard, saliva and blood. "Does this mean I'm your new cabin boy?"

He glared at her. "Aye, and you shall be the best cabin boy I have ever had or I will feed you to the sharks. Savvy?" He turned and stomped back to the ship.

Still assessing the damage done to his breeches and silk stockings, Mr. Montgomery strolled up to Annie. He motioned her to follow Captain Hawke. Annie's pulse raced as she walked up the gangway to join the Realm's motley crew of outcasts and gentlemen.

CHAPTER THREE

It did not take Annie long to find Captain Hawke on the main deck. He glanced at her and then called to a young sailor. "Christopher, this is my new cabin boy. Take Andrés below and have Doc look him over."

"Aye, Aye, Captain." Christopher, a two-year veteran of the Realm, turned to Annie. "Follow me," he said.

Despite a pronounced limp, the sailor moved quickly. Annie followed close behind to the hatch. Not hampered by a dress or petticoat, she could not resist jumping down the last three steps of the ladder.

Annie adjusted her eyes to the dimly lit passageway. "It's like a cave down here."

"You'll get used to it."

Christopher gave her a quick tour. He pointed out the fo'c'sle where the sailors slept, the mess deck where they ate, and Captain Hawke's cabin.

Annie jumped when something black dashed by her. "What was that?"

"He's one of the Realm's cats. Great ratter, that one is."

Relieved, Annie wanted to learn more about the ship. "I thought only King George's Navy had surgeons."

Christopher puffed out his chest. "Only the most profitable merchant ships can afford surgeons. But I doubt they pay Doc much. They don't have to."

"Why not?"

"He never leaves the ship." Christopher bent down and crooked his finger urging Annie to come closer. "After midnight, he walks the main deck from bow to stern and back again, but never when there's a full moon."

Christopher watched Annie's eyes widen before he let out a hardy laugh. "I'm teasing. Doc seldom leaves his quarters except to play chess with the captain. Don't look so worried. He's a cranky one, but harmless."

Christopher knocked on Doc's door. It opened to a man of short stocky build, whose silver hair, mustache and ashen complexion made him look older than his forty-three years. Thick eyebrows hovered over melancholy eyes. He stared at Annie through spectacles of thick glass.

Doc studied Annie's swollen cheek and the droplets of blood dotting the front of her shirt. "Hop up on the examining table. I want to get a better look."

Annie did as she was told, all the while biting her lower lip.

"Open wide, boy."

She dutifully obeyed.

"No loose teeth. Your mouth is bleeding. That is easily fixed." After retrieving a bottle from his cabinet, he dabbed a small amount of dry powder to the inside of Annie's cheek.

Doc took a closer look at her bruised face before looking over his shoulder at Christopher. "How did this happen?"

"He was in a fight."

"Do I have the winner or loser of that altercation?" Doc's eyes trained on Annie while he walked around the table.

"Since he is the captain's new cabin boy, I guess you could say he won," Christopher said.

"Not like the captain to pick one so young. This one actually looks like a cabin boy." He looked down at Annie. "Captain Hawke would rather they be able to fend for themselves. Are you able to do that, lad?"

She shrugged. "I suppose."

"Well, you better."

Annie winced as Doc's finger traced the back of her shirt where blood oozed through the material.

"Christopher, you are dismissed. And you, boy, take off that shirt."

Listening to the door close, Annie didn't move.

"Are you deaf, child? Take off your shirt." The longer Annie remained motionless, the harsher Doc's tone became. "I cannot help you if you won't let me treat your injuries, now, can I?"

Annie watched the corners of his mouth strain into a smile. A new strategy had emerged.

"Do you have a name, lad?"

"Andrés, sir," Annie said while she fidgeted with the hem of her shirt.

"That's a fine name—means brave. My son's name was Andrew."

While Doc retrieved another bottle from the cabinet, Annie quickly unbuttoned her shirt. Once it was off, she pulled it around to her chest before drawing the shirt to her neck. She could not see the shock on Doc's face, but she heard it in his voice.

"You have open wounds and scars running the length of your back. Who did this to you?"

Annie's answer was brief. "Aunt Mary."

"Why would she do such a thing?"

When the question went unanswered, Doc did not press her further.

"This is going to sting," he said while he rubbed an astringent into her wounds.

Gritting her teeth, Annie did not make a sound.

"You are tougher than you look. Now pull your shirt down, all the way. I need to wrap a dressing around your body."

"I'd rather not," Annie said.

"I'm not asking you to take it off, lad. I'm ordering you to take it off."

Annie closed her eyes. As she held the shirt firmly to her breasts, she knew her days as a cabin boy were over before they even got started. Slowly, she slid the shirt down to her waist.

Doc gasped when he saw the chest of a pubescent female and not that of a young boy. "Oh, my, Andrés isn't your real name, now is it?"

She promptly covered herself. "It's Annie—Annie

Moore, sir. I have no place to go. Please don't tell the captain."

He did not reply, but instead gestured for her to remove the shirt again. No sooner had Doc finished wrapping the dressing around Annie's torso, the door opened.

Captain Hawke sauntered into the cabin unannounced.

Annie shot a look at Doc. He stared back and sighed. At least for the moment, she knew her secret was safe.

"Are you going to live, boy?" Captain Hawke asked.

"Yes, sir." With her back to him, Annie quickly threw on her shirt and buttoned it.

"It's 'aye, Captain.' You are a sailor now and you bloody well better talk like one."

"Yes—I mean aye, Captain."

"Since you are going to live, how should we celebrate our good fortune?" Not waiting for an answer, he headed for the door. "Doc, send the boy to my cabin when you are done with him."

As the door slammed shut, Doc and Annie stared at each other. Doc broke the silence. "Where are you from?"

"Surrey County," Annie answered.

"How did you get to London?"

"I snuck a ride in the back of a wagon going to market. The farmer never heard me with all that squawking going on from those chickens, and I had no trouble squeezing in between their cages. I jumped out when he got to the outskirts of London."

"That explains this." Doc plucked a small feather tangled in Annie's hair. "Won't your family miss you?"

"My cousin Erik will, but no one else will."

"There must be someone."

Annie stared down into her lap. "There was Uncle William, but he…he's dead. And I would rather die myself than go back to live with Aunt Mary. She blames me for his death, says I'm cursed." Her voice trailed off.

"Are you?"

"Am I what?"

"Cursed," Doc said.

"Perhaps I am. My beloved uncle is dead and so are my parents and little sister, too. They died during the influenza outbreak in…"

"In 1733, eight years ago," Doc said as he grabbed the edge of the table to steady himself. "That was a bad time, a very bad time.

"I apologize for interrupting you. How did your uncle die?"

"Four days ago, Uncle William was repairing Lord Spencer's stable roof when he fell off. He split his head wide open. Aunt Mary said if it weren't for me, it never would have happened. 'You're cursed', she said. Then she whipped me bad, but I didn't cry. I would never give her the satisfaction.

"Erik said next time, she would kill me. He gave me some of his brother's clothes and then he cut my hair.

He said it would be safer if I pretended to be a boy. Couldn't be an unescorted female in London, now could I."

Doc's brow wrinkled. "Well, you can't very well be an unescorted female aboard this ship, either."

Annie crossed her arms. "I'm not going back to Aunt Mary."

"There must be someone, family or friends, who can take you in."

Annie wanted to say Lord and Lady Spencer, but reality punched her in the stomach. She was maid and companion to their daughter, Abigail, nothing more, nothing less. "There's no one," she said.

The floorboards creaked with each step Doc took. Annie caught two words mumbled under his breath: girl and trouble. He stopped, frowned. Deep in concentration, he paced some more. Again, he stopped. This time he scowled at Annie. "There's one thing for certain, you won't be sleeping in the men's quarters if I have anything to say about it. That would be highly improper."

"Where will I stay then?"

"Here, of course."

Doc watched Annie squirm on the table, her bladder about to burst. He pointed to a stained chamber pot in the corner of the room. "Feel free to use it. I won't look."

"Uh, thank you, but I'll wait until you are out of the room."

"I don't leave these quarters often."

Annie blushed. "That's what Christopher told me."

"But not to worry, it's time I spoke with the captain." Doc proceeded to the door.

Annie slid off the examining table. "Kind sir, please don't tell him I'm a girl."

Doc whirled around. "I am not particularly kind and you had best call me Doc like the rest of the crew does. Remember this, nothing gets past the captain. If he discovers you are a girl, he will have you off this ship faster than you can say, 'God save the King.'"

He smiled. This time, Annie saw it wasn't forced.

"But he won't find out, because I have a plan," he said.

* * *

While waiting for Doc's return, Annie explored his cramped quarters. There was no bed, only a stowed hammock lying next to the chamber pot, now christened with Annie's fresh urine. Books arranged alphabetically were held in place by a one-inch wide wooden slat running the length of a single shelf.

"No Thomas Carew poems here," Annie said while she thumbed through a book entitled *De Morbis Cutaneis: A Treatise on Diseases of the Skin.*

She put the book away and turned toward the medicine cabinet. Pulling open a drawer, Annie looked at its contents, scalpels and scissors. Another drawer contained saws. She picked up one and stared at its serrated edge. Annie realized it was used for hacking off human limbs and not those of trees. She quickly dropped it back into the drawer.

Annie continued to look through the cabinet. The medicine bottles were in snug individual compartments. An object wrapped in velvet was wedged behind one of the bottles. Before she could remove it to get a better look, Annie saw the door swing open.

"Find anything to your liking, Annie?" Doc said as he shuffled in.

"No." She quickly closed the cabinet. "Please, Doc, you can't call me Annie. If I am to have any chance of staying on this ship, you must call me Andrés"

Doc waved his arms in the air. "This is my home. I will call you whatever I wish to call you in my home. Is that understood?"

"Yes." Annie changed the subject. "What did you and the captain talk about?"

"You, of course, his cabin boy."

Goose bumps peaked on her arms.

"The captain is allowing you to sleep here only until your infection is gone."

"You didn't tell me I had an infection."

"You don't, but I told him you did. I said you would never make it to the colonies if I didn't treat it vigorously."

"I'm impressed that you convinced him."

"Oh, I didn't convince him. He is suspicious, but since I have never caused him any trouble, he said he would indulge me in this bit of folly. But you are not to have a hammock."

"It won't be the first time I have slept on the floor,"

Annie said. "I don't care if I have a hammock or not."

"You should care. The captain doesn't want you to have a hammock, because that would be considered permanent. In the meantime, you will sleep on blankets on the floor. You will slide around when we are in rough seas. Not much we can do about that."

"As long as I can stay here, that is all I care about," Annie said.

"And once you are *healed*, Captain Hawke expects you to sleep in the fo'c'sle with the rest of the sailors."

Annie couldn't help but utter a nervous giggle.

"That will never happen. Perhaps, you would like to be a surgeon's mate." Seeing the confused look on her face, he added, "My assistant."

Remembering the saw in the drawer, Annie shivered. "Thank you for wanting me to be your assistant, but I was hired on as a cabin boy. What will my duties be?"

"You will bring Captain Hawke his meals, mine, too, clean up after him, like a manservant."

Annie scrunched up her face. "I don't have to dress the gent, do I?"

"He would box your ears if you tried."

Her cheeks cooled.

"Many of your duties won't involve the captain, like helping the ship's cook."

"So, I'm to be a servant *and* a cook? I thought my life as a sailor would be more exciting?"

"You are not a sailor yet. Just be grateful you have a place to stay."

She ignored his rebuke. "I saw men climbing the masts. Now that would be exciting. I always liked climbing trees."

"I hope you were good at it, because the captain is sending you aloft this afternoon with Christopher. He says he doesn't want you hidden away in the bowels of the ship like me." Doc pulled out a flask from his desk drawer and unscrewed the top. "I told him maybe he should make you a gunner's mate and then you could simply blow yourself up, a less painful death than falling off a mast."

Annie's mouth went dry.

"The captain's not a patient man." The creases in Doc's brow deepened. "Mustn't keep him waiting. Off with you now."

CHAPTER FOUR

While Annie stood outside Captain Hawke's cabin, the soft rumblings of her stomach became insistent roars. She began to tremble. Whether it was from hunger or nervousness, she didn't know. Annie grasped the door handle for support. Her knuckles barely made a sound when she knocked on the door.

No answer. She rapped harder.

"Come in."

The captain's voice didn't sound inviting, she thought. Annie opened the door. She took several halting steps into the cabin before her eyes rolled back in her head as she collapsed on the Turkish rug.

In her dreamlike state, she heard an unfamiliar name called. She heard it again, this time louder.

"Andrés!"

A sharp slap to her uninjured cheek followed. Her head flopped to one side. An even harder slap stung the same cheek. "Leave me alone," was what she wanted to say, but she could only moan.

Annie heard retreating footsteps and then quicker ones returning. She remained motionless on the blue, red and yellow carpet until...

Splash!

Annie sat up with a start. Captain Hawke stood

over her with a dripping tankard in his hand. At first, she did not recognize him without his tricorn hat. She licked the sweet port trickling down her lips before wiping her face on her sleeve.

Captain Hawke's dark eyebrow jutted upward. "Thought I lost my cabin boy before we even set sail."

Annie struggled to focus her eyes.

"You passed out," he said.

With eyes half shut, Annie's nose twitched in the direction of the captain's half-eaten breakfast.

"When was the last time you ate a full meal, boy?"

Her head throbbing, Annie thought a moment. "I can't remember."

He waved his arm toward the food. "Help yourself."

Aware the captain was not helping her off the floor, Annie self-consciously crawled to his desk. She pulled herself into a musty-smelling armchair before reaching for the plate and stuffed her mouth with cold eggs, bangers and mash. She swirled her finger around the dish, wiping it clean of the potatoes. Annie then licked her finger up one side and down the other.

With the food settling in her stomach, Annie looked at the dish and then at the captain. "Oh my, I didn't mean to eat it all."

He laughed. "Keep eating like that, boy, and we'll fatten you up in no time."

"Pardon my poor manners."

He shrugged, leaving Annie to believe he didn't care one way or the other.

While light streamed through the stern-side windows, Annie scanned the cabin. She took it all in. There was an unmade bed securely attached to the wall and floor, a hammock stowed next to it. For rough days out at sea, she assumed. Unlike the surgeon's quarters, the ceiling was high enough for the captain to stand at his full height.

Her attention returned to the desk. Amid rolled charts and maps was an assortment of snuffboxes. One intricately carved box caught her eye. Annie reached for it, and then hesitated. "May I?" she asked.

Captain Hawke dipped his chin.

She picked up the box, turning it about in her hands. She opened and closed the lid. No tobacco. After examining the carved figures of two men holding swords, she said, "It is beautiful craftsmanship, Captain."

Through looking at it, she put the box down on the edge of the mahogany desk and slipped off the chair.

She rested her hand on the corner of the desk. Confident she would not faint again, Annie ventured across the floor. She looked at the sword and knives of various lengths and shapes, some jewel encrusted, displayed on the wall.

But it was the bookcase spanning one side of the cabin that interested her the most. While Captain Hawke's book collection would have filled only a few shelves of Lord Spencer's library, it was imposing nonetheless.

"Have you read them all, Captain?"

"Most of them." Staring at Annie's skeptical face, the captain said, "Does that surprise you?"

"A little. You don't look..." Annie's mouth slammed shut. Her eyes widened.

"Spit it out, boy. I don't look like what? Educated? Is that the word that caught your tongue?" he said. "I am not educated, not like Mr. Montgomery, but I can read. Not many sailors can say that. Can you read, boy?"

"Aye, Captain. I love reading poetry, history. I especially enjoy Shakespeare. I learned my letters at my father's knee, but it was...a friend who introduced me to the Bard." Annie almost mentioned Abigail's name. As it was, she wondered if she had given him too much information.

"Just like I thought; you *are* an educated Englishman. Do you have a favorite book, boy?"

"My mother's poems by Garcilaso de la Vega, she read them to me in Spanish. There was another book I loved, my father's book about pirates. I really loved that one, too, but I can't remember its name."

Annie's hands became hot. She rubbed them on her trousers, but could not extinguish the memory of sifting through warm ashes. None of her treasured belongings escaped the flames, not one dog-eared page, not even a thread from her mother's embroidered sampler. "Aunt Mary burned them all," she said bitterly under her breath.

"Speak up, boy," the captain said.

"It was nothing important, Captain."

He turned and pulled out a book, flipping through its pages. "You said a book about pirates was one of your favorites?" His voice was even, each word measured. He replaced the book to the shelf. "Does a pirate's life sound exciting to you, Andrés?"

"Aye, Captain. When I was much younger, my little sister loved watching me pretend to be a pirate." Annie left out the part about how she battled the imaginary foes while wearing a dress down to her ankles.

With her left arm curved at the elbow, hand pointed upward, Annie playfully thrust her other hand at the captain. "En garde," she said.

Annie froze in mid-thrust when the captain seized her arm, almost wrenching it from its socket. When he dropped her wrist, he spat out his words. "There is nothing entertaining about pirates. When pirates hoist the Jolly Roger, they know they can take what they want. That skull and crossbones put fear into many a sailor's heart. If it didn't, then cannonballs fired across the bow certainly would." His eyes narrowed. "Merchant ships seldom fight back."

Annie rubbed her shoulder. "Why not?"

"They are not adequately armed and the miserable wages sailors are paid doesn't inspire much loyalty."

Annie's curiosity wasn't satisfied. "Is Godenot..."

She barely got the name out when the captain bellowed, "What possesses you to speak of that devil's name on my ship?"

"I-I only wanted to know if he is as evil a pirate as I have been told, worse than Edward Low or

Blackbeard."

Captain Hawke glared at her, his eyes dark as coal. "On the Realm, we speak neither his name or of his ship."

"The Crimson Revenge?" Annie clasped her hand over her mouth, but it was too late.

"Did you not hear me?"

"Please forgive me, Captain. I will be careful not to mention...Well, you know what I mean."

He sighed. "Do you have any more questions?"

His voice had softened. Annie took it as a peace offering. She felt it safe to ask, "If the Realm was attacked, would you give up without a fight?"

The captain's eyebrow peaked higher than she had witnessed before. "Never!" He slammed his fist down on his desk barely missing the snuffbox Annie had admired earlier. "*My* men are handsomely paid and we have enough cannons to blow any pirate ship to bloody hell!"

His chest heaved in and out. "Enough about pirates," he snapped. "If you want to take a book back to Doc's quarters, take one."

Annie nodded as she scanned the books.

"I don't have all day, pick one."

She ran an uncertain finger along the tomes' spines.

Impatient, Captain Hawke pulled out a book of poetry by John Dryden. "Don't care much for his writing." He pulled out another. "Here's one about the Roman Empire, conquests, murder. That should satisfy a curious lad such as you."

"Thank you, Captain."

He strolled to the door. "After you clean my cabin and take my dishes to the galley, come topside. Time you met your shipmates."

CHAPTER FIVE

On the quarterdeck, Captain Hawke chatted with Mr. Montgomery. When he saw Annie, he called to Christopher, "Show Andrés around and tell him about ship protocol."

"Aye, aye, Captain. Come along, Andrés."

"What is protocol?" Annie asked Christopher as they crossed the deck.

"Ship etiquette," he replied.

Annie knew what etiquette meant, but could not fathom how it applied on the Realm while she watched a Jack-tar spit tobacco juice over the rail. Another bare-chested sailor scratched his sweaty armpit.

"What kind of etiquette are you talking about?"

"No stealing, fighting or gambling." Christopher then whispered, "There are plenty of wagers made on just about everything on this ship, but you don't want the captain to catch you."

"What happens if he does?"

"No one's been caught."

"Is there anything else I should know?"

"The first mate is called Mr. Montgomery or sir. The bosun is Mr. Allan and Doc is Doc. The rest of the crew will let you know what to call them."

Annie tilted her neck back to watch a sailor scale

the ratlines leading to the top of the mast.

"That's Baggott," Christopher said. "He's a good man, in his twenties. He came aboard with his best friend, Carter." He gestured toward a sailor who appeared to be working with the rigging. "Like the rest of us bosun mates, Baggott and Carter are mighty friendly. I cannot say the same for the gunners. Ready to do battle, they are, but you won't meet them. They live on the gun deck."

"What do you mean they live on the gun deck?"

"They eat and sleep down there. They are all top-notch, too. Have to be, since the captain refuses to sail in convoys under the Royal Navy's protection."

"Why not?"

"Captain Hawke trusts no one's authority but his own. Besides, it would slow the Realm down. He has a reputation to keep." Christopher stopped for a moment near the ship's bell. "What do you think of the captain?"

Annie ran her hand along the belfry. "He's… interesting. But I dare say, he keeps a messy cabin."

"I know," Christopher said. "I used to keep it tidy for him."

"Were you his cabin boy?"

"Aye, but I haven't been one since I became a full-fledged bosun mate about a couple months ago. That's why the captain needs a new cabin boy."

"I always thought cabin boys were much younger. That Lawrence chap was certainly no child. How old were you when you became his cabin boy?"

"Sixteen. I am eighteen now." Christopher smiled

while his boots clicked unevenly on the deck. "It is no secret Captain Hawke doesn't want to deal with children."

"Why does he hire cabin boys at all?"

"I don't know." Christopher chuckled. "But I can tell you this; the crew is mighty surprised Captain Hawke chose you."

"I guess I am just lucky." Annie smiled. "Finish showing me around, Christopher."

He pointed his finger. "The bow is the front of the ship."

Annie cut him off. "And the stern is the back. Starboard is the right side facing the bow and larboard is the left side." Annie reveled at the astonished look on Christopher's face.

He scratched his head. "Well I'll be. This isn't the first time you been on a ship, now is it?"

"A coble, my father's fishing boat. It even had a sail, a small one."

"Ah, so you're a fisherman's son."

Annie made exaggerated rowing movements with her arms. "Salt water in me veins. Quite exciting bringing in the day's catch, you know." Annie remembered how her father had taken her a handful of times on his boat when the sea was calm. She knew of no other girls allowed that privilege.

Christopher continued telling Annie the terminology she was not familiar with. "The bulkheads are what you call walls. The bulwark..."

Preoccupied with Christopher's dissertation, Annie

didn't see the sailor swinging a mop handle at her legs. The quick blow to her shins pitched Annie forward. Her outstretched hands broke her fall, knees banging on the deck. Before she could get up, a wave of cold water splashed over her backside sending a spasmodic shiver through her body. Quickly rolling over, she found herself looking up at a short burly sailor glaring down on her.

"Look what you've done!" He snarled.

"What I've done?" Annie fired back.

In one hand, the sailor held an empty bucket. With the other hand, he poked a mop handle into her stomach. "Ye prissy little maggot, clean up this mess!"

Annie grabbed the handle, shoving the mop back at him, but the sailor pushed back with even greater force. Fearing he would impale her, Annie yielded. "I'll clean it up."

Once on her feet, Annie clutched the mop. Cursing under her breath, she furiously swabbed the deck until Mr. Montgomery marched up and grabbed the mop out of her hands. He tossed it back to the sailor.

"Mr. Symington, you're not being kind to Captain Hawke's cabin boy, now are you?" he said.

Symington shuffled his feet. "I was only 'aving fun with the little maggot. I meant no 'arm, sir."

"No harm done, Symington, but don't let it happen again. And for future reference, the boy's name is Andrés, not maggot."

"I will try to remember, sir, but me memories not like it used to be," he said as he thumped the side of his head with the mop handle.

"Go about your business, Symington."

Symington glowered at Annie as he ambled off.

Mr. Montgomery dismissed Christopher and led Annie out of earshot of the crew. "Stay out of Symington's way."

"He's not very friendly," Annie said.

"He doesn't have to be. Symington is the Realm's carpenter. He and his mates keep us afloat." Mr. Montgomery placed his hand on Annie's shoulder. "Another thing, lad, don't go crying to the captain. You will receive no sympathy from him."

"I don't cry, sir." She shrugged off his hand. "Never have, never will. It is a waste of time if you ask me. I don't tattle either."

"I think you are going to do just fine on the Realm. However…" Mr. Montgomery studied Annie from the top of her collar to the bottom of her soaking wet breeches. "You need some seafaring clothes, Andrés. Now, where did Christopher run off to?"

Annie pointed toward the bow of the ship where Christopher was polishing the ship's railing.

Mr. Montgomery tossed the lanky sailor a drawstring purse. "Since there is no time to make Andrés any clothes, see if you can find the boy some proper ones in town. Get him a sea bag as well. Any money left over, get something for yourself, but be prudent."

"Aye, Mr. Montgomery." Christopher turned to Annie. "Come along, Andrés."

CHAPTER SIX

While Annie walked alongside Christopher on the bustling London street, two sailors approached. She hoped her instincts were wrong, but the men looked like they were up to no good.

The two looked at each other, then separated. They quickly came up on either side of Annie and Christopher. Without so much as a how-do-you-do, one pushed Annie aside before both sailors bumped their shoulders into Christopher. Helplessly, Annie watched the youth plunge backwards.

"Watch where you're going, mate," the shorter of the two dark-eyed sailors said to Christopher lying on the ground.

The other one jumped on Christopher, pinning him to the ground. Christopher made no attempt to fight back while the sailor mussed up his hair with his knuckles.

"What you looking at?" The sailor hollered when he saw Annie staring down on him.

The sailor's olive complexion was several shades darker than hers, his accent distinct, but from where, Annie wasn't certain. She looked at the sailor standing behind the one straddling Christopher. Brothers, she wondered as she looked at their black hair.

Panic rose in her chest. "Leave him be," she said. To her dismay, what she wanted to sound like an ultimatum came out more like a request.

The one not holding Christopher shoved his fist in her face. "What you goin' to do about it?" he asked.

The other let go of Christopher and joined his companion. They circled around their smaller prey. Grins erupted on each of their faces.

They blocked Annie's escape. One of them seized her shoulder whipping her around to face him. She balled her hand into a fist just as Christopher bounded to his feet.

"That is Andrés de la Cruz, mates," Christopher announced while he smoothed back his greasy blond hair. "He's Captain Hawke's new cabin boy."

The sailor holding Annie immediately let her go as both men backed off.

Christopher's composed manner puzzled Annie. "You know them?" she asked.

"Aye," Christopher said. "They're from the Realm."

The tattooed sailor extended his hand to her. "You're a little one, Andrés de la Cruz."

Annie had no intention of shaking his hand until Christopher told her it was okay.

"I'm Joao Perreira, but everyone calls me Perry. Rodrigues and I are two of the Portuguese aboard the Realm."

"So, you are Christopher's shipmates." Annie said. She wiggled her fingers trying to get feeling back after Perry's crushing handshake.

"We are your shipmates, too," he said as he eyed her up and down.

"Don't worry. I am getting Andrés some seaworthy clothes," Christopher said.

Perry smiled. "Bom—good!"

While the two sailors wandered off, Annie looked back just in time to see Rodrigues put Perry in a choke hold. Watching their tangled bodies wrestle on the edge of the road, she asked Christopher, "Do you like to fight?"

"I am not much of a fighter, but I know you are. I watched you on the wharf. We all did." He threw a fake punch at her.

Annie ducked and pointed to her black eye. "I'm really not much of a fighter."

* * *

Annie had no say in what was bought during her shopping expedition. Christopher held up a shirt or a pair of canvas trousers in the air. He would eyeball her and the clothes and decided if they would fit or not. Then Annie stuffed each item into her first purchase, a sea bag.

"Should I get some different shoes?"

"No, yours will do. Most sailors go barefoot, don't slip as bad on the deck," Christopher said while he tied a red scarf around his neck. He admired it and his new belt buckle in the reflection of a storefront window. "Change into your clothes, Andrés. You should return to the ship a sailor, not a landlubber."

"You want me to change...here?"

"No." He pointed to the alley. "There."

"You won't peek. Will you?"

"Peek? Why would I do that? I don't want to see your naked arse." Christopher said as he squared his shoulders and pulled out a knife. "I will guard the entrance from drunkards and thieves." He planted his feet firmly in an uneven stance. "Do I look threatening, Andrés?"

Except for his height, there was nothing threatening about Christopher, Annie thought. She managed to look quite serious when she answered, "Aye, you look mighty fierce."

She saw by his grin that her answer pleased him. But then again, she thought, everything seemed to please Christopher.

Annie couldn't wait to get out of her damp clothes. She pushed aside debris in the alley, making enough room in the filth for her and the sea bag. The overwhelming odor was worse than the alley she had spent the previous nights in. Holding her breath, she threw off her shirt and put on the new one. She did the same with the trousers which, to her disappointment, were a tad looser fitting than her cousin's had been. Nevertheless, she appreciated the freedom of the clothes, no confining corset or hem to catch a heel on.

Unable to hold her breath any longer, Annie sprinted from the alley. She laid the sea bag next to her and pulled her boots back on. When she was through, Annie paraded in front of Christopher, showing off a white and blue checked shirt. She then put on a warm fearnought jacket. Her trouser cuffs, rolled several times above her slim ankles, revealed thick grey stockings, and a knitted Monmouth cap covered her dark hair.

"Do I pass inspection, Mr. Christopher?"

"Aye, you're a fine looking tar, except...."

She crossed her arms over her chest wondering if she weren't flat enough. "Except for what?"

"How you walk."

"What are you talking about?"

"I can't explain it, but it is kind of like..." He hesitated. "You kind of walk like a girl."

"A girl, you say. And how exactly does a girl walk?"

"Something like this." Christopher demonstrated. His hips swayed from side to side in an awkward fashion while he fanned himself with one hand.

She burst into laughter. So did Christopher. Annie wasn't sure how she walked, but one thing for certain; she didn't walk like Christopher.

"Oh, please, I do not walk like that. But even if I did, then everyone had better get used to it. I am who I am. Nothing is going to change that."

"I know what you mean." Christopher looked down at his boots, one two sizes larger than the other.

Annie tried not to gawk and changed the subject. "No more of this silliness, Christopher." She hiked up her trousers. "I am eagar to return to the ship."

CHAPTER SEVEN

Bundled in her fearnought jacket and red cap, Annie again hiked her trousers above her waist as she boarded the Realm. While she watched the sailors prepare for the next morning's departure, Christopher chatted on about what she could expect from her first day out at sea.

Fascinated with the sailors loading and securing casks and bales in the holds, Annie heard little of what Christopher said.

She listened to the chorus of deep voices. "Together!" Using an assortment of pulleys, slings, and ropes, the sailors labored to the rhythm of their chanteys.

She turned to Christopher. "Were you saying something?"

His shoulders sagged. "Nothing important."

"Andrés," called Mr. Montgomery. "Vast improvement, lad."

He then looked up into the cloudless sky. "And if there is any inclement weather this fine day, you most certainly are prepared. What is your opinion, Captain Hawke?"

Annie turned to the unhurried footsteps coming up behind her and snapped to attention.

Captain Hawke studied her over-sized clothes. "Hmm, are you hiding contraband under there?"

His eyes then drifted from her jacket down to her stockings which were slowly disappearing under the rolled cuffs of her trousers.

When Annie realized her trousers had slipped past her hips, she reached under her jacket and tugged up on them. To her relief, they had not reached the point of no return.

Captain Hawke shook his head. "You don't have any meat on your bones, boy. Why didn't you get yourself a belt?"

"Couldn't find one small enough, Captain," Annie said.

"We can't have you going around with your trousers falling down around your ankles; now can we? Sailors mend their own clothes. You better be good with a needle and thread."

"I have sewed on a button or two. Me mum was a seamstress," Annie said.

"Your cuffs, hack 'em off." Captain Hawke said.

She cocked her head. "Uh, pardon me, Captain."

"Don't roll up your cuffs; hack 'em off," he repeated. "And where's your knife?"

"Christopher didn't say anything about a knife, Captain." Annie didn't want to get Christopher in trouble for the oversight; but with the captain obviously annoyed, she wasn't about to make her life any more complicated than it already was.

The captain noticed Annie admiring his ivory

handled knife. "You like my knife, boy?" Captain Hawke said.

"It is quite handsome, Captain. I have never seen a knife handle carved like a monkey before. And are those ruby eyes?" she asked.

"That they are. Some people believe monkeys are good luck."

"Are you one of those people?" Annie asked.

"No. I don't believe in that superstitious nonsense."

"Tell Andrés how you got the knife, Captain," Christopher said.

"You tell him, Christopher," Captain Hawke replied.

Christopher didn't need any more encouragement. He told the story at break-neck speed. "An old sailor named Mason Rain had taken a liking to him." Christopher pointed to the captain. "They were shipmates when Rain said that one day his knife would be his." He again pointed to the captain. "Rain made good his promise, but not the way he thought he would. His knife was no match against a flintlock pistol."

Annie whispered, "The captain shot him?"

"No, he didn't shoot Rain. Another sailor did, and then that sailor took Rain's earrings. Gold, they were. And while that murderous fiend emptied the old man's sea chest, the captain, who wasn't a captain at the time, rolled Rain's body over and took the knife. It was rightly his, you know. I didn't leave anything out, did I Captain Hawke?"

The captain suppressed a yawn with his hand. "You about put me to sleep, lad."

Christopher looked at Annie. "It is better when Symington tells it. Now, he's a good storyteller."

"Christopher, here's a story you can tell the crew," Captain Hawke said. "It is the one about the captain giving his lucky knife to his curious cabin boy. See what you can do with that one."

Captain Hawke then unsheathed his weapon and handed the knife, handle first, to Annie.

She waved her hands in protest. "Captain, I cannot possibly accept anything of such value."

"You saw my knife collection. This one is nothing more than a mere trinket, and you need a knife."

Christopher leaned down to Annie. "He never was that generous with me. I would take the knife if I were you. You are going to need all the luck you can get."

"It didn't bring Mr. Rain much luck, now did it," Annie murmured.

Mr. Montgomery broke in. "Accept the captain's generosity and be done with it."

He turned to the captain. "However, the boy needs a knife belt that fits him. Don't you agree, Captain?"

"You are quite correct, Mr. Montgomery. Mr. Allan can make the boy a proper knife belt. Until then, it stays with me."

"Thank you, Captain. I won't be needing it soon; will I?" Annie asked.

CHAPTER EIGHT

Annie knotted the last stitch and pulled on the scratchy trousers. Without Abigail's freestanding cheval mirror, Annie had to rely on how the trousers hugged her hips rather than how they looked on her. She yanked down on the sides. A snug fit, she thought.

"Doc, what do you think?"

He glanced up from his cup of tea and inspected her work. "After the captain sees those stitches, he will send you off to repair sails."

Annie hoped Doc meant that as a compliment.

Banging on the door startled them both. While Annie grabbed her cap off the table, Doc wiped off the hot tea that splashed onto his hand.

"Captain Hawke wants Andrés on the quarter deck!" An unfamiliar voice shouted.

Annie quickly pulled her cap down over her ears. She scurried through the passageway and up the ladder.

She skidded to a halt at Captain Hawke's feet.

He inquired in a gruff tone, "Will this be your first time at sea, boy?"

"No, Captain, I am a fisherman's son." The half-truth came out easily.

"Am I to presume, then, that you have your sea

legs?"

"Aye, Captain. I won't be getting seasick if that is what you are worried about."

Seeing his raised eyebrow, Annie wondered if he doubted her. His next words confirmed her suspicions.

"Perhaps, it is you who should be worried. I have seen your hands, Andrés. It has been a long time since you fished on anyone's boat. Tomorrow, after you have spewed your guts over the side, you will begin your duties; but for now, Christopher will show you how to climb the mast."

As if he were swatting at an annoying fly, he waved her off with the back of his hand.

* * *

Annie stood at the bottom of the foremast watching Christopher maneuver the ratlines.

"What you waiting for!" he yelled down at her.

Grasping the lines, each one more than a foot apart, Annie sucked in her breath. While she made her ascent, the thick lines dug into the palms of her hands and the soles of her feet.

"Don't look down!" Christopher shouted.

"You are!"

"I have done this a thousand times. Look at the lines in front of you, nothing else."

Annie concentrated on the lines. She clung to them in a death grip, putting hand over hand. She wished there were tree limbs to caress her shoulders or leaves to brush against her cheek, but only a cool breeze greeted her through the crisscrossed lines.

When she reached the yardarm attached horizontally across the mast, a gush of air poured from her lungs. "I made it."

Christopher offered her his forearm. "That you did, Andrés. Hold on. Ready?" His tongue ran along cracked lips as he helped her onto the yard. "If you get dizzy, close your eyes and don't let go."

Annie had no intention of closing her eyes. They were wide with awe. Safely on the yardarm, she marveled at the perfect view of sailors finishing their day's labor and of ships dotting the harbor. "It is amazing up here, Christopher."

"I know. I never tire of it. It is even more amazing when you are swaying with the wind in a storm."

"I will take your word for it," Annie said as she looked at Christopher's sea-ravaged face. Running the back of her fingers across her smooth cheek, she wondered how long it would take her face to be etched like his. "Did you always want to be a sailor?" she asked.

"Not always. But when my father died of consumption, I knew I had to take care of me mum. I could have been a cabinet maker like Father, but I decided to make my fortune out at sea."

"Have you made your fortune?"

He laughed. "Not a fortune, but I have never regretted my decision. On my first day on the Realm, Captain Hawke ordered *me* to climb the mast. Symington said what everyone was thinking, 'Why did the cap'n hire a cripple to be his cabin boy?' But I proved myself."

"From what I have seen, nothing slows you down, Christopher. Looks can be deceiving."

He laughed. "Aye, look at you."

"Uh, what do you mean?"

"You are stronger than you look. I didn't expect you to climb the ratlines so fast. You are barely winded," he said. "Now it is my turn to ask you a question. Have you always loved the sea, Andrés?"

"Always," she said.

Annie remembered standing in frigid water up to her ankles with her mother by her side, prying limpets off the rocks for bait. Memories flooded her mind: the fishing nets, coiled ropes, her father's coble hauled to shore. Her recollections abruptly ended at the shrill sound of the bosun's pipe.

"Mr. Allan's piping orders. Best you be off, too, Andrés," Christopher said.

"Aye, I'll follow you down," Annie replied.

"No, you go first. Don't want you landing on top of me if you should lose your grip."

Annie's stomach tightened. "I hope you are joshing me."

Christopher's ready smile was nowhere to be seen. "I take my safety seriously, Andrés. Have to take care of me mum, you know."

Annie gulped hard. "Meet you at the bottom," she said with as much enthusiasm as she could gather.

CHAPTER NINE

With Christopher and the crew off celebrating their last night in England, Annie explored the lower decks of the Realm alone. Since Symington was gone, her first stop was the carpenter's storeroom. She quickly became bored with the tools of the trade: axes, hammers, nails and various items she did not recognize. From there, she went to the area of the ship that she was most interested in, the abandoned gun deck.

The low ceiling and stale air made for a less than hospitable environment. On both sides were eight cannons, all nine pounders, sitting on eight sturdy elm carriages. Christopher had explained earlier to Annie that the weight referred to the cannonballs and not the cannons. She ran her hand over one of the balls. She pictured gun ports swinging open, a pirate ship off in the distance. But a draught board, its game pieces scattered under a hammock, reminded her that the gun deck was not only a place to do battle, it was home to forty-eight sailors.

Out of the corner of Annie's eye, she saw movement. She suddenly realized she wasn't alone. The hammock hanging above the draught board was occupied. A dark figure, not particularly big, emerged in front of her. One foot plopped down and then the other. His smile revealed teeth filed into sharp points. When he blew out the candle in her hand, Annie took it as her cue to run.

She dropped the candle holder and sprinted to the ladder. Annie expected the man to be on her heels and drag her back, kicking and screaming, to his lair. Instead, she heard only maniacal laughter fading in the distance.

Once she caught her breath and her heart stopped pounding in her chest, Annie decided to check out a safer place, the mess deck. Perhaps, she could join in the camaraderie of at least a few sailors eating and swapping stories.

To her disappointment, Annie found only the ship's cook, Mr. Waverly, sitting on a bench secured to the deck.

"Has everyone gone ashore?" Annie asked.

"Most of them," Mr. Waverly said as he scooped mash and peas onto the back of his fork. "Only you, Doc, and the men on watch will be eatin' my fine cookin' tonight."

"When will you be going ashore, Mr. Waverly?"

"I am too old for that foolishness. Besides, I have no one to go home to. Not like some of the men, who will be spending their last night with the missus and their brood."

"What about Mr. Montgomery? He sure was all fancied up this afternoon, and he smelled real good." Annie tried not to blush.

"All I know is that the first mate won't be downin' sour whiskey at The Black Anchor Pub. He'll be doin' somethin' more suitable for a fine gentleman like himself.

"He is nothin' like the captain, you know, but they are closer than two babes in a mother's womb." Mr. Waverley wagged his plump finger at Annie. "Now don't go tellin' no one I said that."

"I promise, Mr. Waverley, I won't."

"Ah, you are a good lad, aren't you?" he said as he pushed a bowl of blackberries toward her.

Annie took a handful of the berries and plopped them into her mouth. They were not as sweet as she would have liked, but they were tasty, nevertheless.

"I didn't have a chance to ask Christopher where he was going," she said

"Visit his mum if he has the time is my guess."

"So, he won't be going to a tavern."

Mr. Waverly shrugged. "I didn't say that, but if he does, he will be outta there as soon as the fightin' starts."

"And the captain?"

"The captain will have a lady on his arm, maybe two. No strumpets, mind you. He has better taste than that. He has quite the eye for the ladies and they have quite the eye for him," he said with a wink.

"How do you know?"

The old cook spread his beefy arms and scanned the mess deck. "More stories are told here than in the fo'c'sle. Only most of these ones are true."

* * *

Annie placed a tray of food she retrieved from the galley on Doc's desk.

"Have you eaten?" he asked.

"A little."

Doc yawned as he pierced a piece of roast beef with his fork. He looked up from his plate. "Long day tomorrow, you need to turn in early."

"I will."

Annie couldn't sleep any better than she could eat. Staring into the darkness, she listened to Doc's snoring that all but shook the bottles in the medicine cabinet. Annie kicked off her blanket and crept out of the cabin.

On the quarterdeck, she sat cross-legged watching sailors returning from their night of celebration. Some staggered aboard. Their shipmates carried others, bloodied from fighting or in drunken stupors.

A cheery voice called out from the shadows, "Do you want company, lad?"

Annie jumped to attention. "Certainly, Mr. Montgomery."

"Relax, boy," Mr. Montgomery said. "Are you excited about tomorrow?"

"Aye, sir." Even in the dim glow of the lanterns, Annie saw his well-tailored clothes were still in pristine condition. He definitely had been celebrating in a more dignified manner than his fellow shipmates had been.

"Want to play a game, Andrés?" Mr. Montgomery asked.

Annie tilted her head. "A game, sir?"

"Just something to pass the time. Are you interested?"

Annie nodded. "Yes, sir."

"All right then. Pick a sailor and tell me about his life before he became a member of the Realm."

"But I don't know most of them."

"You don't have to. Guess what their story is. For instance, see that fellow over there? He signed on while I had business in town."

The young man Mr. Montgomery referred to was in his late teens. Unlike most of the sailors, his black hair hung below his shoulders. Rolled-up sleeves revealed muscular arms.

When he introduced himself to Annie earlier in the day, he had taken her breath away. "His name is Ambrose Barrette," Annie said. "But he prefers being called Barrette."

"He is certainly a brawny fellow, no doubt a blacksmith's apprentice," Mr. Montgomery said. "I'd wager he was too friendly with the blacksmith's daughter. Her father then chased Barrette out of town, and that is the reason he is now a member of our fine crew."

"That is amazing, sir. Christopher told me that Barrette was a blacksmith's apprentice. But I don't know about the rest of your story. How do you know if you are right or not?"

"I don't. But whatever Barrette's story is, the possibilities are high that he is running away from someone or something."

Wise or not, Annie could not resist asking the first mate, "What would my story be, Mr. Montgomery?"

"Hmm, let's see." The first mate studied Annie. "The clothes you wore when I first saw you weren't yours. You have had a good life as well as a bad one. You should not be well educated, but you are. You are a paradox, lad."

"How often are you right?" Annie asked.

"Often enough."

"If you don't mind me saying, sir, you are a paradox as well."

The jovial first mate's smile disappeared.

"I am guessing you are an Oxford gentleman, and you should be the owner of this vessel, not her first mate. You are as indebted to the captain as he is to you. How did I do, sir?"

Mr. Montgomery's brow knitted together. "You play the game well…well, indeed. Now go below and get some sleep, busy day tomorrow."

CHAPTER TEN

"Time to get up!"

Annie pulled the blanket over her head. "What time is it?"

"Four bells."

"Four what?" She said groggily while she stretched her arms.

"Four bells," Doc repeated. "It's the way sailors tell time."

"Maybe you can explain it better to me than Christopher did."

"The striking of a bell represents thirty minutes. There are eight bells, one for each half hour of a four-hour watch. Right now, it is four bells, six o'clock, two hours into the morning watch."

Annie shot straight up. "The captain wanted his breakfast two hours ago!"

"He is too busy to worry about eating now. I am surprised Mr. Allan's confounded whistling on that pipe of his didn't wake you."

Annie heard the Realm buzz with activity. Looking up at the overhead, Doc tapped his lips twice. "I am accustomed to all kinds of movement and sound down here. I know when the ship changes course and how bad a storm is without feeling a drop of rain."

He tapped his lips a third time. "But that racket—I just don't know."

Wearing the same clothes from the night before, Annie folded her blankets and pulled on her knitted cap. "I think it's quieted down," she said. "I'll take a look."

"Wait!"

It was too late. Annie opened the door. At the sound of rushing footsteps, Doc pulled her back and quickly closed the door as Ambrose Barrette dashed by.

Annie pressed her ear to the door. She trembled as Barrette cursed his pursuers. After a brief struggle, an uneasy silence followed and then voices boasted of their catch. Annie backed away from the door when she heard what sounded like a body being dragged down the passageway. She and Doc stared at the door as the minutes passed like hours. Annie could wait no longer. Against Doc's protests, she again went for the door. He grabbed her arm, but she pulled free and opened the door a crack. Convinced the passageway was clear, she ran to the hatch.

* * *

On the main deck, Annie found Captain Hawke waving a piece of paper in the face of a rotund man. He was significantly shorter than the captain. His soft-looking hands and elegant clothes convinced Annie that he was not a sailor.

"My first mate paid you handsomely, Mr. Collins," Captain Hawke said. "I don't care what this paper says."

Annie's eyes drifted toward the wharf. A shiver of horror shot through her. Not only was Barrette hunched over in shackles, but Christopher as well. She saw Christopher's lips form the word *NO* as Barrette spat in a captor's face. The man, his arms thicker than Annie's slim waist, struck Barrette's bloodied head with the butt of a pistol.

As she watched Barrette crumble to his knees, Annie turned to Mr. Allan. "Are they going to kill them?"

Mr. Allan clenched and unclenched his fists. "No, Barrette and Christopher won't do the press gang much good if they're dead."

"I don't understand," Annie said.

"They force men into service for the Royal Navy," Mr. Allan said. "When Collins' men came aboard the Realm, the captain had me signal the crew. But it was too late for Christopher. They had already grabbed him. Barrette came to his aid, but the lad is no fool. When he saw he was outnumbered, he took off running like the rest of the sailors."

Mr. Allan patted Annie's shoulder. "Don't worry. You are safe."

Annie turned when she heard the captain shout, "We had a deal!"

"As you can plainly see by the press warrant, Captain Hawke, my hands are tied. The Royal Navy needs more sailors. I shan't allow you to interfere with my job simply because you are not loyal to The Crown," Collins replied.

65

Mr. Montgomery pushed past Mr. Allan and joined in the fray, "What about your loyalty, Mr. Collins? How many bribes have you taken from other captains to secure their crews' safety?"

"My loyalty is not in question, Mr. Montgomery." Collins tapped his snuffbox. "Personally, I thought you and Captain Hawke would be pleased I took the lame one off your hands. We took twenty men off the Legacy yesterday. All able-bodied, I might add. But if you are not grateful, perhaps I should take more." He leered at Annie. "Starting with this young chap."

Captain Hawke stepped between Mr. Collins and Annie.

"The Royal Navy needs strong, seaworthy *men*," the captain said. "Why would you want my cabin boy or Christopher? Even you called him lame,"

Collins smirked. "How much will you pay to get him back?"

"You despicable little man!" Captain Hawke shouted.

Collins sniffed a pinch of tobacco up each nostril. "It's business, Captain Hawke, nothing more, nothing less."

"Mr. Montgomery will compensate you, Mr. Collins. However, you are never to step foot on my ship again. I would hate to see misfortune befall you."

Captain Hawke's biceps bulged as he grasped Collins under his armpits lifting him off the deck. The man's stumpy legs dangled in space.

"Put me down!"

"With pleasure!" The captain said as he hurled him into the railing.

Collins bounced off the wooden rail before falling in a heap. Two of his men pulled out knives, but when Mr. Montgomery stuck a pistol to Collins' temple, he called them off.

Having sustained nothing more than a bruised ego, Collins struggled to his feet. He retrieved his powdered wig, placing it lopsided on his head.

In his haste to collect payment from Mr. Montgomery, Collins did not see a black ledger fall from his coat pocket, but Annie did. More importantly, so did Captain Hawke.

CHAPTER ELEVEN

Christopher returned to the ship without fanfare.

Symington complained to no one in particular, "The cap'n gets the cripple back and loses the fit one."

Annie reached up to Christopher's face and just as quickly pulled her hand away. "You're bleeding," she said

He brushed her aside as he walked across the deck. "Captain, we must do something!"

"What do you suggest, Christopher?"

"Rescue Barrette," he murmured.

"Say it again, Christopher. Only this time, say it like you mean it."

Christopher straightened and in a clear voice said, "Rescue Barrette, Captain."

"Now, that is more like it," Captain Hawke said.

* * *

After consulting with Mr. Montgomery, Captain Hawke had the ship's carpenter brought to him.

"Symington, you will be in Mr. Montgomery's rescue party," the captain said while he ripped out all references to the Realm from Collins' ledger. "I assume you are up to it."

"Aye, aye, Cap'n! Ye know me, always ready for a fight!"

"Be quick about it, or we sail without you. Understood?"

"Understood, Cap'n!"

"Good." The captain turned to Mr. Montgomery, handing him the monogrammed black ledger. "Give this to the proper authorities. Most of Collins' dealings are illegal."

"So, we are to rescue Barrette *and* give this to the authorities," Mr. Montgomery said while he skimmed through the pages. "Is there anything else you would like us to do? Perhaps, we should bring back feed for the livestock or maybe a new knife for your collection."

"Are you through, Mr. Montgomery? You have contacts, use them." Captain Hawke continued. "Symington, Mr. Allan, Carter and Samuel Baggott are experts with pistol and blades. They will all be in your rescue party. "

"Is it wise sending Mr. Allan and his best bosun mates?"

"Actually, I have decided you will be taking two more. Smitty and Christopher will accompany you as well," Captain Hawke said.

"I can understand Smitty, but why Christopher? Why not a gunner? Now, that would be a good pick."

"Christopher is as capable as any sailor, and he is good with a knife."

"He carves blasted little sea creatures. And if Barrette hadn't tried to rescue Christopher, he would not be in this fix."

"Exactly, Christopher needs to return the favor."

"You are insane."

"You know better than to question my judgment... or my sanity." The captain said with a crooked smile.

"This is a foolhardy mission and you know it. We should have rescued Barrette when he was still on the dock."

"Collins' men were prepared to fight. This time, we will have the element of surprise on our side. Even my cabin boy knows about the element of surprise."

The captain looked at Annie. "What unites a crew more than a foolhardy mission?" Captain Hawke asked.

"A *successful* foolhardy mission," Annie replied.

"I like the way you think, boy," said the captain.

Mr. Montgomery grumbled as he went off to gather the six members of his rescue party.

* * *

While the first mate gave words of strategy and encouragement to his men, Annie watched Christopher nervously whittle away on a piece of wood.

"My condolences mate," Symington mumbled.

"What are you talking about?" Christopher asked.

"Doubt ye will be making it back, son. But don't worry, I will make sure ye 'ave a proper burial."

"Oh, *I'll* make it back, Symington. But I am not certain you will," Christopher said. "Do you want a burial at sea or should we simply plant you in the ground?"

It pleased Annie to see Symington speechless.

CHAPTER TWELVE

The ship came alive in its final preparations to weigh anchor. With Mr. Allan gone, Perry piped the captain's orders to the remaining rigging crew. Annie watched the quick movement of the bosun mate's hand —open, shut—as he signaled the crew.

The soft hairs on her arms stood on end when Captain Hawke commanded, "Andrés, when I give the order, hoist the Blue Peter. Rodrigues, show him how it's done."

"Aye, Aye Captain," said the dark eyed sailor. "Come along, Andrés."

Annie followed Rodrigues while the deck crew moved in seamless precision. Annie awaited further orders.

After the sails came out of hiding like giant butterflies emerging from their cocoons, Captain Hawke shouted, "Hoist the Blue Peter!"

No sooner had Annie raised the blue and white flag, a hush came over the crew. It had obvious significance, she thought. Seeing the sailors' reaction, she asked Rodrigues, "Why is everyone so quiet?"

"The Blue Peter signals those on shore that we are about to sail."

"But we can't sail. The rescue party hasn't

returned."

"Don't worry. They will see the Blue Peter," Rodrigues answered.

"Make yourself useful, boy. Go aloft and be our lookout." Captain Hawke pointed to the barrel-shaped structure lashed to the top of the main mast. "And take this."

Annie tucked the spyglass into her waistband before scrambling up the ratlines. Once on the platform, she held the glass to one eye surveying the streets leading back to the ship.

It was not long before she shouted, "I see Smitty and Mr. Allan!"

A roar came over the Realm as the sailors crowded the larboard rail. Minutes later, she yelled another name, "Barrette!"

"How does he look?" Rodrigues yelled up at her.

"Good!" After his ordeal, Annie thought, he looked mighty fine. Her eyes trained on him as he dashed across the dock with head held high.

Her heart skipped a beat. "Christopher!"

The gangly youth ran awkwardly toward the wharf. Once aboard, Christopher's fellow shipmates good-naturedly slapped him on the back.

Annie spied yet another sailor.

"Symington!"

Waving his cutlass in the air, Symington marched on board as if he were leading a parade.

As much as she detested the man, Annie was glad to see he was returning safely. After all, he was still one of her shipmates.

Annie's palms became sweaty when she saw no more sailors approach the vessel. Celebration turned to quiet concern, except for the captain who remained calm at the helm.

She wiped her hand on her trousers before bringing the spyglass back to her eye. "Mr. Montgomery!" Annie shouted.

Cheers rang out while sailors flung their caps into the air.

Mr. Montgomery stopped at the edge of the wharf. Resting his hands on his thighs, he glanced over his shoulder. No one else came into view.

Annie watched with dismay as the gangway was pulled onto the ship after Mr. Montgomery raced on board.

Captain Hawke's command, "Cast off!" reverberated in Annie's ears. The Realm swung away slowly from the wharf.

She didn't put down her spyglass until she saw the last two sailors. "I see Baggott and Carter!" she yelled, her voice hoarse. "Carter's hurt!"

With the ship heading out to sea, Annie knew neither Baggott nor Carter would be joining their shipmates. That fact was not lost on the crew either. Their work chanteys sounded more like dirges sung at funerals.

Annie stashed the spyglass back under her waistband. While she descended the ratlines, she kept her eye on Baggott and Carter, best friends when they came aboard and now best friends about to share the same fate. Undoubtedly, Annie thought, they would soon be joined by a very angry press gang.

Given no further orders, Annie continued to watch the two sailors stranded on the wharf. Baggott unwound his arm from around Carter's waist and patted his friend's back. Carter stared straight ahead as if he were facing a firing squad. Annie gasped when Baggott suddenly rushed behind him and shoved Carter over the edge. The sailor tumbled forward, arms and legs flailing in the air before disappearing beneath the murky water. Baggott dove in after him.

Annie held her breath until she saw Baggott break the surface clutching Carter. He had wrapped his arm under Carter's chin and with his free arm, attempted to swim to the ship. But Baggott made little progress with his panicky friend.

Annie's heart sank until she heard Captain Hawke command, "Heave to!"

The Realm began to slow.

She watched Mr. Montgomery remove his shirt, boots, sword and pistol before plunging off the side of the ship. Annie couldn't imagine anyone surviving a dive from that height, but he made it look easy.

Only when Mr. Montgomery swam to the two sailors, did Baggott relinquish his hold of Carter. Baggot took several gulps of air before swimming toward the rope ladder dropped over the side of the ship.

Mr. Montgomery struggled to avoid Carter's

thrashing arms. Annie was amazed at how much strength the sailor still had as he blindly fought Mr. Montgomery's efforts to save him.

She held her breath when both slipped under the water. Just when Annie believed it was a losing battle, they reappeared. Apparently, Mr. Montgomery wasn't taking any chances as he slugged Carter in the jaw. No longer having to fight the sailor, Mr. Montgomery headed back to the Realm with Carter's limp body in tow.

As soon as Baggott and Smitty hauled Carter onto the deck, Captain Hawke remarked, "Can't have too many rescues in one day, now can we?"

Annie noted a hint of a smile on the captain's face. "You had no intention of leaving them behind, did you, Captain?" Annie said.

He answered simply, "There will be plenty of tall tales spun in the fo'c'sle this evening."

"Doc says I shouldn't go to the men's quarters at night. He says it is too rowdy for one as young as me."

"Poppycock. Tonight, you will join your shipmates in the fo'c'sle. You answer to me, not to Doc."

"Aye, Captain," Annie said, even though she knew differently.

CHAPTER THIRTEEN

With the wind in her sails, the Realm surged through the choppy sea. Veteran tars moved across decks and through passageways as if they were on dry land. While Annie struggled to synchronize her steps with the up, down motion of the ship, she felt like a child learning to walk for the first time.

Not trusting her stomach, Annie ate little all day. An hour into the evening's second dogwatch, she joined the crew gathered in the fo'c'sle to hear the account of Barrette's rescue.

In his booming voice, bare-chested Ainsworth announced, "Make room for Barrette, Mr. Allan, Smitty, Symington, Christopher, Baggott, and Carter!"

Their shipmates bowed in exaggerated respect as each member of the royal court of seven entered. Cheers of "Huzzah!" rang out when freckle-faced Carter limped in with the help of Baggott.

Led by the striking Ambrose Barrette, the sailors took their places on sea chests laid out for them. Barrette swept his black hair away from his swollen left eye. He listened to the questions fired at them: Did they put up much of a fight? How many did you kill?

Except for the creaking of the ship, the fo'c'sle fell silent. Mr. Allan nodded to Symington. The sailor gazed about his audience with yellow-tinged eyes.

The hair-raising tale began. "There were twenty, maybe fifty of them press men. All fearless, and armed to the teeth they was. What we lacked in numbers, we made up in—what's the word?"

"Determination?" Smitty suggested.

"Aye! Determination. Anyways, Mr. Montgomery..." Symington paused and looked off toward the passageway where the first mate stood leaning against the bulkhead.

"Don't let me stop you, Symington," Mr. Montgomery said. "I will be discussing the day's events with Captain Hawke. Carry on."

Symington craned his neck, making certain Mr. Montgomery was gone before he resumed his tale. "Mr. Montgomery gave the order to attack," he said. "There 'e was, ready to do 'is business, pistol in one 'and, sword in the other. But the lads all stayed back shivering in their boots. Shivering they was, 'til *I* comes forward to lead the way. With one swoop of me trusty blade, three 'eads went rolling—all three wide-eyed and looking mighty surprised." As Symington batted his eyelashes for added effect, the crew broke into uproarious laughter. "That's 'ow Carter got 'urt. Tripped over one of them 'eads, 'e did!"

Violent pitching and rolling of the ship abruptly ended Symington's tale of Barrette's rescue. The bow to stern, larboard to starboard movement sent sailors toppling into each other. Others dove into the safety of their hammocks.While the ship's bell clanged, Captain

Hawke and Mr. Montgomery barked orders. With his experienced bosun mates, Mr. Allan scrambled up the ladder to the hatch.

Annie searched madly for a bucket. Sliding and swaying, she saw Barrette in the same predicament. A forceful roll of the ship slammed Annie into the bulkhead. Thankful her head hadn't split open, Annie continued her search for a bucket. She succeeded— only to have Barrette rip it away from her.

Barrette dropped to his knees burying his face in the rusty pail. When there were no more retching sounds, he handed it back to her. Careful not to breathe in the foul odor, she positioned it under her chin.

She saw Barrette's cheeks puff out like a squirrel's full of nuts. He tried to snatch back the bucket, but she held on tight. The ship once more rolled to starboard, sending her toppling onto Barrette. With the contents of the bucket spilling out, Annie emptied her stomach onto Barrette's shoulder.

CHAPTER FOURTEEN

Doc watched Annie inch her way into his cabin, "What on earth happened," he said as he rolled out of his hammock. He steadied himself. "Didn't I tell you it wasn't a good idea going to the fo'c'sle at night."

"The storm is the problem, not the fo'c'sle, Doc."

Taking a whiff of the odor filling his quarters, he realized what had happened. Helping Annie take off her clothes was no easy task as the ship continued to pitch and roll. He bundled her in a blanket before throwing the foul smelling clothes out into the passageway.

"Am I going to die?" She groaned. "Just tell me. I can take it."

"No one dies from being seasick. You will ride out this storm like the rest of us. Lucky it's not a bad one."

Not a bad one? Annie wondered how much worse it could possibly be.

After Doc cleaned Annie up, they waited for the storm to pass. He spent the night on the floor with blankets swathed across his shoulders while Annie was tucked safely in his hammock.

The next morning when she poured herself out of the canvas, the steady rocking of the Realm sent her back with the dry heaves.

* * *

Keeping his voice low, Christopher stood in the doorway. "The captain wants to know—any improvement with the boy?"

"A little. Andrés drank some of the broth you brought earlier."

"Shouldn't he be well by now? It has been two days."

Doc sighed. "It is one of the worst cases of seasickness I have seen."

One eye peered over the edge of Doc's hammock. "I'm not deaf, nor am I dead. I can hear you."

Christopher walked through the doorway. "You need to get better, Andrés. I am doing your work as well as my own"

"I am trying to get better," Annie said. "Is that another book from the captain?"

Christopher placed Daniel Defoe's *Captain Singleton* on top of the growing pile of books on Doc's desk. He then handed Doc Annie's clean clothes. They still had a lingering odor to them.

"Christopher, can you get me some water?"

"Who do you think I am, Andrés, *your* cabin boy?" Christopher feigned indignation as he took a mug off Doc's desk. He helped Annie take a sip.

"How is the rest of the crew, Christopher?" Doc asked.

"A few are still sick. Nothing like Andrés, though." He looked over at Annie. "But you're a strong one. I don't care what Symington says."

"What is that old blow-hard saying this time?" Annie said.

"You don't want to know."

CHAPTER FIFTEEN

The next morning, being careful not to wake Doc, Annie opened the door. Weak, but grateful her headache was gone, she leaned against the bulkhead every few steps. She slowly made her way to the mess deck.

Finishing their morning meal, sailors sat at one of two long tables. Except for a few glances in her direction, they barely acknowledged Annie's presence.

She settled for the empty table. Like the benches, it too was secured to the deck. Annie ran her hand along the table's raised edge that kept the tin dishes from sliding off. Doubtful she would be able to eat, Annie was about to leave when Barrette got up from the other table, bringing with him a plate of food.

He looked at her gaunt face and sunken eyes. "You are as gray as Mr. Waverly's socks. Sit." He handed her a bruised pear. "You need this more than I do."

She stared at the pear for a moment before taking it. Annie took a bite of the partially eaten fruit. She chewed until the pulverized piece slid easily down her throat.

"Are you mad at me, mate?" he asked.

"Why would I be mad at you?"

"Taking the bucket from you."

"Oh, that. All is forgiven."

"Forgiven, am I? Saved your miserable life, I did."

"And how, pray tell, did you save my life?" Annie asked.

"You landed on top of me instead of on the hard deck."

Annie rolled her eyes at him.

"You won't tell the captain I took the bucket from you. Will you?" Barrette asked.

"Why would I?"

"To get me in trouble."

"I wouldn't do that. Besides, I think we are even. I threw up all over you."

Barrette laughed. "You're right. Shake on it?"

Annie reluctantly took his hand. He quickly turned hers palm-side up.

"Mighty smooth hand for a fisherman."

She pulled her hand away. "How did you know I was a fisherman?"

"Christopher told me," Barrette said before he grabbed her hand back, giving it a crushing shake. "How long were you a fisherman...a day?"

"None of your business."

Barrette turned his attention back to the food on the table. "Try the hardtack," he said. "It will be easy on your stomach. Careful, you don't break a tooth on it."

Annie cautiously bit down on the unsalted biscuit. "When did you get your sea legs, Barrette?" she asked.

"The next morning after the storm."

"Have you gotten to climb the mast yet?"

"Aye, but first, Mr. Allan put me to work mending sails. Then I had to listen to his boring speech on the importance of properly tying knots."

"Knots?"

"Mr. Allan takes his knot tying very seriously." Barrette flashed Annie a grin. "I, on the other hand, take nothing seriously."

Annie continued talking to the charming sailor when Smitty wandered into the mess deck. Taking one look at her, he broke into a jig and danced his way across the room.

"I won!" he yelled to the group of sailors sitting at the table. The lean sailor proceeded to collect a prized star knot from one of the men and an irritated look from another tar who grudgingly handed over a ring to him.

"What's going on?" Annie asked.

Barrette laughed. "He must have won the bet."

She took another bite of the hardtack. "What bet?" she mumbled.

"Some of the sailors made bets on when you would get your sea legs...or die." Barrette replied.

"Die? Were there many bets made on that one?"

"Only one."

"Let me guess," Annie said as she looked across the room. "Symington must be very disappointed that I am still alive."

"Watch out for him."

"I have been told that before. I can take care of myself," Annie said. "Did you bet?"

"I don't make sport of someone else's suffering, unless he has a bucket in his hands and I need it." Barrette again smiled, then strode out of the mess deck.

Annie sighed. She hated seeing Barrette leave.

Samuel Baggott came up behind her. He stared at the half-eaten fruit sitting by her hand. "Are you going to eat that?"

"You can have it." It was the first time she had seen Baggott up close without his cap. She stared at his tight red curls.

"No one else in my family has red hair," Baggott said before popping the rest of the pear into his mouth. "That is what you are staring at, isn't it?"

"I was just thinking about my sister, Sarah. She had red hair just like yours." Annie could not remember the last time she had spoken Sarah's name out loud. Just saying it stabbed at her heart.

Baggott smiled. "Welcome aboard sailor," he said as he walked off.

She could not believe the pleasure the word sailor brought her.

Annie downed the rest of the hardtack and was about to leave when Symington confronted her. He gripped her arm so tightly; the blood stopped flowing to her fingertips.

"Ye owe me, boy. I lost me 'ard earned wages because of ye."

"That is too bad, Symington, but perhaps you should not have bet on me dying. It is my understanding that Captain Hawke frowns on gambling on his ship." Annie hoped Symington didn't see the beads of sweat dotting her forehead. "Speaking of the captain, he is expecting me," Annie said.

Symington let go of Annie's arm. Baring his teeth, he sneered. "Don't want to keep the cap'n waiting, now do we."

CHAPTER SIXTEEN

"About time you got your sea legs, Andrés. Report to Mr. Allan," Captain Hawke said in a curt tone.

Receiving no compassion for being seasick from the captain, Annie replied back just as curtly, "Aye, Aye, Captain." His slightly raised eyebrow was enough to satisfy her.

Annie found Mr. Allan at the foot of the foremast. Of medium height, the trim bosun had strong shoulders and wavy brown hair.

When Mr. Allan saw Annie, he began his speech. "The rigging relies on the mastery of knot tying. The operation of the sails determines the direction and speed the ship travels."

As he droned on, Annie was convinced he had given the same speech for years to all inexperienced sailors.

Out of Mr. Allan's field of vision, Barrette crossed and uncrossed his arms each time Mr. Allan did. Annie found it no small feat not to laugh, which she was certain was Barrette's goal. Apparently, she thought, he was not joking when he said he took nothing seriously.

"Any questions?"

Annie shook her head. "No, sir."

Mr. Allan looked over his shoulder at Barrette.

"Demonstrate for the lad how to tie a bowline and a square knot."

"Aye, aye, sir."

Now with his back to Mr. Allan, Barrette made faces at Annie, all the while showing her how to tie the two knots. She chuckled while her nimble fingers copied his.

"This is serious business, Andrés. Do you find it amusing?" Mr. Allan asked.

"No, sir, not at all." As she continued tying the knots, Annie ignored Barrette.

Mr. Allan went on with his talk. "The brail is a smaller line that draws a sail in or out. While we have pulleys to do some of the work, you will be expected to go aloft to adjust lines and sails as well. Climbing a mast while we are docked is quite different from climbing one at sea. The wind will whip right through you and a sail can knock the best sailor off if he loses his concentration. Are you up to the task, Andrés?"

"I most certainly am, sir."

"If you feel you are not up to it, you can tell me. You don't want to put yourself or your fellow shipmates in danger." Mr. Allan gazed up at the topsail and looked back at Annie. "Again I ask you, are you positive you are up to the task?"

Barrette broke in, "Beggin' your pardon, sir, but Andrés had been seasick for several days. He might not be strong enough to climb the mast."

His jaw taut, Mr. Allan asked Annie, "What do you say to that, Andrés?"

"I am fine, Mr. Allan—never felt better." Annie turned to Barrette and whispered, "I thought you said you didn't take anything seriously."

When she turned back to Mr. Allan, he was shaking his head.

"It is no secret you have been seasick, Andrés. I did not intend to send you aloft today. I hoped you would make the right decision. Unfortunately, you didn't. I will send you aloft when you can show better judgment and not before."

Captain Hawke had been eavesdropping on the conversation. "Andrés! You are working in the galley today," he shouted.

"The galley?"

The captain's dark eyes narrowed. "Aye, the galley, or perhaps you would prefer spending the rest of this voyage in irons."

With each of his steps toward her, Annie dragged her feet two steps backward.

"What will it be? Irons or the galley," he said.

"The galley, Captain."

"At least you have made one wise decision today," he replied.

* * *

Annie found refuge on the lower deck. "Barrette needs to mind his own business. First the bucket, now this! I'm glad I threw up all over him," she said. "I couldn't have done worse than if I were on a bloody pirate ship!"

Consumed by anger, Annie didn't hear Symington

coming behind her. Without warning, he picked her up and pinned her against the bulkhead.

"Are ye daft, boy? It is cursed to talk about such matters on a ship, 'specially this one!"

Annie slid down the wall. Dazed, she rubbed her neck and head. "Why this ship?"

Symington pointed up at the overhead. "Cause 'e was one," he said as he spat on the deck, barely missing Annie's foot.

"Who?" she whispered.

"Who da ye think? The cap'n, of course."

"The captain was a pi…?"

Seizing Annie's right arm, Symington lifted her off her feet and slapped his other hand across her mouth. "Yer a slow learner. Aren't ye?"

"Symington!"

The sailor dropped Annie as he reeled around. His hefty body was more agile than Annie thought possible.

"Cap'n 'awke!"

"What is going on here?"

"Nothing, Cap'n. I was only 'elping the lad after 'e took a nasty fall," Symington said while he dusted off Annie's shirt and trousers.

"Is that what happened, Andrés?"

She pushed Symington's hands away. "Aye, Captain, he was helping me."

"You're dismissed, Symington." Captain Hawke said.

Symington sauntered off saying under his breath.

"Remember what I said, boy."

Captain Hawke turned to Annie. "Would you care to tell me what *really* happened?"

"I fell, Captain. Just like Symington said I did. I am a bit clumsy at times."

"Symington is a great storyteller. You, on the other hand, are not." Captain Hawke frowned while he studied her face. "What did you think of his fable about Barrette's rescue?"

"Was any of it true?"

The captain shrugged. "With Symington's stories, there is always an element of truth in them."

"Always?" she asked.

The captain folded his arms. "I thought I assigned you to the galley."

"I was heading that way when..." Annie hesitated.

"When you tripped?" Captain Hawke said. "Make sure you don't trip again. Next time, you might not be so lucky."

CHAPTER SEVENTEEN

With flour caked under her fingernails from a day's work in the galley, Annie skimmed the pages of *Captain Singleton*. Unable to concentrate, she read the same words over and over again. Finally, she gave up and laid the book down.

"Your first day as a sailor did not go well, did it?" Doc said.

"Who told you?"

"No one had to. If it had gone well, you would be chattering away like a magpie. Do you want to talk about it?"

She took a deep breath. "Barrette told Mr. Allan I should not go aloft today."

"After having been seasick, you were actually going to climb the mast? It sounds like this Barrette fellow has more good sense than you do."

"I was a good climber before we went out to sea," she said through clenched teeth.

"Yes, before you went out to sea and before you had taken ill."

Annie bit her lip. "I want to be accepted by the other sailors. I want them to like me."

"Getting yourself or someone else killed is not the way to do it."

Annie frowned. "Let's change the subject."

"What do you want to talk about?" Doc asked.

"I have an excellent idea. Let's talk about you." Annie rolled over and rested her chin on the back of her hands. "What did you do before you came on the Realm?"

"I am not an interesting subject," he said.

"Please." Annie puckered up her lower lip making Doc smile.

"How can I resist that sad face?" He took a deep breath. "I studied at Edinburgh University before becoming a surgeon at St. Thomas's Hospital in London."

There was a long pause that Annie realized was going to be permanent. "Don't stop there," she said.

Doc took a swig from his flask. "That is where I met Roger Moon. We became best friends. He had a little sister." Softly, almost prayerfully, he said her name, "Emily."

"Were you in love with her?"

"I still am."

"Is she pretty?"

"Not pretty, beautiful. Have you ever seen storm clouds open up to reveal the sky when you peer into the heavens? That glorious blue was the same color as her eyes. You are a lot like her. She always spoke her mind. Her father said it was unladylike to discuss politics or religion, but that never stopped Emily."

"Did you court her?"

"You are so much like her, full of questions." Doc

peeked above his spectacles. "Over the years, I watched her grow from a lovely girl to a beautiful young woman. I married Emily when she was eighteen. I was thirty-two. When I proposed to her, I never thought she would say yes. I will never forget her words. 'Arthur Cromwell, I have loved you forever. Yes, I will marry you.'"

Doc went to the medicine cabinet. Moving aside a bottle, he pulled out an object wrapped in velvet, the same one Annie had seen the day before the Realm set sail. He solemnly uncovered it to reveal a miniature portrait painted on ivory. He ran his finger ever so carefully across its smooth surface. He handed it to Annie.

"This must be Emily. Oh, Doc, she is absolutely beautiful," Annie said as she gave it back to him.

For a moment, the portrait brought life to Doc's sad eyes. Again, he ran his finger across her likeness before returning the tiny portrait to the cabinet with his trembling hands.

"Where is she now?" Annie asked.

"She died in 1733."

Annie shuddered. "That is the same year…."

"I know, the same year you lost your family," Doc said. "I lost everyone I loved in that epidemic. Me, a doctor, could not save my own…" His voice faltered.

Barely above a whisper, Annie said, "You told me you had a son named Andrew."

His eyes downcast, Doc said, "Yes, I had a son named Andrew and a sweet daughter as well,

Beatrice."

"I am so sorry, Doc," Annie said. She wished she could say more, but couldn't. Kind words hadn't helped her when she stood behind a stone church watching her father, mother and baby sister being lowered into their graves. She knew no well-intentioned words could take away the pain.

Silently, Doc extinguished the candle.

CHAPTER EIGHTEEN

Three days' worth of grease clung to Annie's clothes. Delivering meals to the captain's cabin had been her only break from working in the galley.

"Good evening, Captain Hawke." Annie kicked the door shut with her foot as she balanced the cumbersome dinner tray in her hands. "Good evening Mr. Montgomery."

Sitting at the gate-leg table, the first mate touched the tip of his nose with his finger. "Flour," he said.

"Oh." Annie put the plates down with a clatter before wiping off the smudge with her sleeve. "Is it gone?"

Mr. Montgomery nodded.

"Andrés did you cook these chickens?" Captain Hawke asked.

Annie forced a smile. "No, but I plucked them."

The captain leaned back in his chair. "Mr. Waverly is quite pleased with your work in the galley. In fact, he wants you to work there for the remainder of our voyage."

"Captain, I beg of you, I would rather die than pluck another chicken as long as I live."

"And to think, I thought you had found your life's work."

"Jonathan," Mr. Montgomery interrupted. "Don't tease the lad. Tell him."

Annie placed the back of her hands on her hips, then realizing how she must look, put her arms by her sides and shifted her weight onto one leg. "Tell me what?"

"While 'tis true Mr. Waverly is pleased with your work, Mr. Allan is even more impressed with your knot-tying skills. Tomorrow, after you have tidied up my cabin, you will report to the bosun." He shook his finger at her. "Don't do anything rash this time."

"Oh, no, Captain. I promise I will behave myself, and I will eat two bowls of porridge so that I am extra strong to climb the ratlines. And…"

"Whoa, boy. He said nothing about sending you aloft."

Annie thought a moment. "Whatever Mr. Allan wants me to do, it will be better than working in the galley. No offense to Mr. Waverly." This time Annie's smile was genuine as she refilled the captain's and Mr. Montgomery's tankards with Taylor's Port. "You won't regret this, Captain."

"I had better not." Captain Hawke clanked his tankard with Mr. Montgomery.

"Can I get either of you gentlemen anything else?"

"No, we are fine," Captain Hawke said.

Annie walked toward the door. She looked at Captain Hawke over her shoulder. "Will you be playing chess with Doc this evening?"

"Aye." His eyes fixed on Annie's cap. "Andrés, take

off your cap. There has not been a spit of rain. Besides, you have not been outside for days."

"I will remove it if you wish, Captain, but I have grown quite fond of it."

"I see." Captain Hawke stroked his short beard.

"Let the lad be, Jonathan," Mr. Montgomery said. "At least Andrés isn't running around half-naked like Ainsworth. I have often wondered if that sailor even owns a shirt."

Annie cleared her throat, trying hard not to laugh. "If there isn't anything else, Captain, I will be on my way," she said as she opened the door. "Enjoy your chess game with Doc."

CHAPTER NINETEEN

Captain Hawke hunched over the table, staring intently at the chessboard. A smile crept across his face as he moved his bishop. "Checkmate."

"Ah, good move," Doc said. "When are you going to play a game with Andrés? I have been teaching him, you know. He is a quick learner "

"Speaking of the boy," the captain said. "It is time he moved into the fo'c'sle with the rest of the crew. His *infection*, if he ever had one, must be gone by now."

"Andrés stays with me!"

Captain Hawke could not hide his astonishment at the outburst coming from his mild-mannered friend. "Since when do you give me orders?"

"When it comes to Andrés' safety, I will do whatever is necessary."

"What does this have to do with Andrés' safety? All I said was that he needs to move into the fo'c'sle."

Doc fidgeted with a chess piece. "I apologize, Jonathan. It's just that given the lad's frail build and his tender age, I feel it better he remains with me."

"I know you have grown fond of the lad, and I must admit, so have I, but if he is ever to become a true member of the crew, he needs to eat, work, and, yes, sleep with the men. You are not doing Andrés any favors by coddling him, Doc. He will never become a man if he stays with you."

"Trust me, Jonathan, whether I coddle Andrés or not, that child will never become a man."

Captain Hawke drummed his fingers on the table. "Pray tell, why is that?"

"I-I mean it won't be safe for him to stay in the fo'c'sle."

The captain's eyes narrowed. "Unless you can come up with a better reason, then Andrés sleeps in the fo'c'sle tonight."

Under his breath, Doc muttered, "Andrés is a girl."

"What did you say?" Captain Hawke gripped the table, his knuckles white.

"Andrés is a girl," Doc repeated.

"Did I hear you say...girl?"

"Yes, I said girl."

The captain's eye twitched. "How long have you known?"

"I've known since the first day she came on the Realm."

"You knew Andrés was a girl, and you kept this from me? Whatever possessed you to do such a thing?"

"And what would you have done? Put her off the ship?"

"You lied to me!" The captain swept his hand across the chessboard, scattering the playing pieces across the floor.

"I never lied. You wanted me to look the child over. I did. Her aunt had brutally whipped her. She had nowhere to go, Jonathan. What was I to do?"

"And what am I to do? Have you forgotten that sailors are a superstitious lot? When they find out there is a girl on board, I will have a mutiny on my hands."

"The sailors are not all superstitious," Doc said.

"Enough are, and it takes only one superstitious tar to discover that Andrés is a girl; then fear will spread like wildfire, and it will be Symington who stokes the flames. Her luck cannot last forever."

"Luck has nothing to do with it. How many times have you told me that Andrés is a tough one, a little scrapper? She has even stood up to Symington. If she stays with me, it is less likely the crew will never find out she is a girl. And from what she has told me, the men don't suspect a thing."

"Not true."

"What do you mean, not true?"

"Matthew has stopped rumors about Andrés being a girl. They started shortly after she first came aboard. How could I have been so stupid?" Captain Hawke looked Doc straight in the eye. "There is no way she can keep up this masquerade."

"With her chest bound, I believe she can," Doc said.

The captain's twitch returned. "You mean she..." Captain Hawke cupped his hands over his chest.

Doc nodded.

"How can that be? She is a mere child."

"She is a fifteen year old child, Jonathan."

Captain Hawke looked incredulous. "I thought she was twelve or perhaps thirteen."

"I beg of you, Jonathan, don't send her away," Doc pleaded.

"I cannot very well put her adrift; now can I?" Captain Hawke's voice dripped with sarcasm.

"So, she stays?"

He bent over and scooped the queen off the carpet. "For now she stays."

"I suppose you will have to tell Matthew."

"Do you really expect me to tell my first mate that I was fooled by an imp of a girl hiding in plain sight? He would never let me live it down. Besides, the fewer people who know, the better."

He ran the back of his hand across his chin. "What is her name? On second thought, don't tell me."

He looked at the queen in his palm before snapping his hand shut. "If this is to work, I must think of her only as Andrés."

CHAPTER TWENTY

"Who won?" Annie asked as Doc shuffled into the cabin.

"I believe I did."

"Unless it was a stalemate, either you won or you lost."

He thought a moment. "The captain won, but I did have him in check."

Eager to hear all the details, Annie urged him on. "Tell me about every move."

"Not tonight, Annie. I'm too tired."

"You had no one in sickbay today, and you played chess with the captain. How can you possibly be tired?

"Trust me, Annie, I am tired."

"You're tired." She folded her arms. "Well, I'm bored. The men sing and carry on in the fo'c'sle each night, and here I sit, either reading or listening to you snore."

"End of discussion, Annie," Doc said.

"We didn't have any discussion," Annie complained.

But Annie was determined to see for herself what went on in the men's quarters. If no one saw her, she thought, Doc would be none the wiser.

Once Annie knew Doc had fallen asleep, she

opened the door. She stopped when the hinges squeaked. Hearing his snoring resume, she edged into the passageway.

She tiptoed to the fo'c'sle and peered inside. The world she saw was more captivating than anything she could have imagined.

Standing in the shadows, Annie winced as Rodrigues pricked a Jerusalem cross onto Perry's forearm. When he rubbed gunpowder into the bloody tattoo, she bit her lip.

She listened to Symington's colorful tale, this one about ships being lured to their doom by sea nymphs. After he finished his story, Annie watched Mr. Allan and Carter duel with their fiddles. Bows flew across strings while the crew joined in boisterous singing. Smitty tapped rhythms on anything he could beat his hands on, including Ainsworth's bald head. Barrette threw down a losing hand of cards to join a group of sailors dancing a jig.

Annie dove behind a water barrel when she heard scurrying sounds. She saw it was only the ship's cat chasing a rat. Relieved no one was coming off his watch, she softly tapped her foot to the lively music.

When a hush came over the fo'c'sle, she caught her foot in mid-tap. Annie left her hiding place. All eyes were on Samuel Baggott, the young sailor with the tight red curls and boyish good looks. He rose slowly from his sea chest and closed his eyes. His haunting melody of sailors lost at sea wafted through the musty air.

Annie crept back to her hiding place. Her eyelids heavy, she hugged her knees close to her chest. His song reached the depths of her soul. Not anxious to return to Doc's quarters, she murmured, "I will stay until the last note is sung."

CHAPTER TWENTY-ONE

Annie stretched her arms high into the air. "Doc, I had the most wonderful dream."

"Oh, did you, now? Want to tell me about it?"

Annie's eyes flew open. She found herself enveloped in a hammock. "Barrette, how did I get here?"

She peered over the edge of the canvass before throwing her legs over the side and tumbled out.

"When I got off the middle watch, I saw your foot sticking out from behind a barrel. I tried to wake you, but you are a sound sleeper," he said. "You mumbled somethin' about 'the last note sung', whatever that means. Anyways, I put you in the empty hammock.

"This morning, I overheard the captain and Mr. Allan talking about you and it wasn't good. I thought you should know."

"I can only imagine how angry Captain Hawke and Mr. Allan must be with me. They must be wondering where I am. I had better go topside."

"Angry? Did I hear you say I must be angry with you?"

Startled, Annie turned quickly to the voice in the passageway. There he stood, the captain—tall, his hands hidden behind his back. A less than happy expression graced his face.

"Captain," she said. "I am truly sorry I didn't bring you your breakfast this morning. It won't happen again."

"See that it doesn't happen again, and you are late in reporting to Mr. Allan. He is less than pleased with you." Captain Hawke's furrowed brow underscored his irritation. "And since when do you bunk in the fo'c'sle?"

"It is all a misunderstanding."

"Misunderstanding or not, you will assist Mr. Waverly today."

"But Mr. Allan wants me to mend sails."

"That is not a request Mr. de la Cruz. That is an order."

Annie twisted the button on her shirt, almost ripping it off. "I said I was sorry."

The captain's left eyebrow shot up significantly higher than the other. "Keep a civil tongue, boy, or maybe you would prefer I confine you to quarters and I mean Doc's quarters, not the fo'c'sle!"

"That won't be necessary, Captain."

"You will work in the galley all day. Is that understood?"

"Aye, aye, Captain."

"Carry on!"

As Captain Hawke stormed off, Barrette made an observation. "The captain's got a bee in his breeches this morning, now doesn't he? But I think he is more angry because you slept here, than not bringing him his breakfast or mending sails. What do you think?"

Annie shrugged her shoulders and proceeded to the passageway. But Barrette was right, she thought. Her having slept in the fo'c'sle did bother the captain. It made no sense. After all, she knew the captain wanted her to sleep in the men's quarters. Like Mr. Montgomery, Captain Hawke was proving to be a paradox, as well.

"I am not the only one who questions it," Barrette hollered after her.

"Question what?" Annie said over her shoulder.

"Why you don't sleep in the men's quarters."

"I have injuries, infected, I am. Doc needs to tend to them," Annie quickly responded.

"You look mighty healthy to me. Besides, Carter's knee still bothers him and it's been said that Ainsworth has a flaming rash on his privates." Barrette shivered as if he were in a cold draft. "They're not all sleeping in Doc's cabin; now, are they?"

Despite the reddening of her cheeks, Annie giggled. "On his privates, you say?"

"You find that amusing?"

"I was thinking about all of us crowded in Doc's cabin. Doc, me, Carter, Ainsworth...his rash."

Not being able to contain herself, she convulsed in laughter.

"It's not funny!" Barrette couldn't contain himself either. He bent over, his hands on his muscular thighs and joined Annie in a moment of hilarity, but it was only a moment. He straightened, the broad grin erased from his face. "Why don't you sleep in the fo'c'sle?" He asked a second time.

"I told you," Annie said.

"I don't believe you."

"It is my age. Doc says I am too young," she blurted out.

"So, which is it, your injuries or your age?"

While Barrette's steady gaze drilled through her, Annie stared right back at him. "My age, definitely my age."

"What are you, twelve? I heard you might even be fourteen. You are old enough to sleep in the fo'c'sle if you ask me."

"I don't recall asking you anything, Barrette."

"There's also been talk that you might be a girl."

"A girl? Nonsense!" Annie turned on her heels and charged Barrette. Her fist rebounded off his firm stomach.

Undaunted, Barrette continued, "Symington calls it nonsense, too."

Annie's eyes narrowed at Barrette. "Symington would never say that. He would be the first one to spread lies about me."

Barrette shook his head. "You are wrong. When he overheard Smitty tell Ainsworth, 'Andrés walks like a bloody girl', Symington cuffed him about his ears and said, loud enough for everyone to hear, 'None of that nonsense; ye 'ear me?'"

"You are good at imitating Symington, Barrette. But I absolutely cannot believe he defended me." She couldn't help but think that made even less sense than Captain Hawke being angry with her because she slept in the fo'c'sle.

"Defending you has nothing to do with it."

"But you said…"

"He is a superstitious old sea dog; that's what Symington is. He says if you were a girl, this ship would be at the bottom of the sea by now." Barrette cleared his throat, again imitating Symington. In a raspy voice an octave lower, he said, "Mind ye, I 'ave no use for the little maggot, but the boy is what 'e is— short, puny, but I wager 'e's tougher than the lot of ye."

"I am flattered to have such an unlikely ally," Annie said. She then glowered at the broad-shouldered sailor standing before her. "You Barrette, what do you say?"

"Me? I suppose I agree with Symington," Barrette said as he absently brushed a strand of ebony hair dangling across Annie's forehead.

"You suppose?"

As if singed by a hot flame, Barrette yanked his hand away from her face.

Annie pushed the errant strand back under her cap. "Would you like me to drop my trousers to prove I am a boy?"

"I am waiting."

"I was joking," Annie said.

Smiling, Barrette replied, "I'm not."

Annie ran her thumbs along the inside of the waistband. "Remember this, Ambrose Barrette; if any tars come in here, it was your idea. Sailors gossip like silly old ladies at afternoon tea. I can see their tongues wagging now. Doesn't bother me, though. It is *you* who sleeps in the fo'c'sle, not I." Hoping she had called his bluff, Annie gripped her waistband. "Here goes."

To her relief, Barrette shouted. "Wait! That won't be necessary. I agree with Symington. You are no lady."

She grabbed the hammock's rope to steady herself as she watched Barrette rush out of the fo'c'sle. "That was close," she said to the cat sashaying against her leg. "I will be more careful next time and not fall asleep."

For the next week, Annie successfully eavesdropped on her shipmates. She returned each night to Doc's quarters after the last note was sung.

CHAPTER TWENTY-TWO

The Realm sat dead in the water, not a breeze to fill her sails. Captain Hawke made an unpopular decision. All the sailors, except for the gunners and Mr. Waverly, took turns manning the longboats. For two days, the crew hauled the ship through calm waters like ancient Greeks pulling a Trojan horse.

After going over the day's events with the captain, Mr. Montgomery said, "You are riding the men too hard. They cannot spend another day rowing."

"And what do you suggest, Matthew?"

"We wait. The winds will pick up."

"We both know that boredom can be the worst enemy at sea. The men need to stay busy. Keeps them out of mischief."

* * *

Meanwhile in the crew's quarters, tempers flared.

"Agony, it is! Look at me 'ands. Blisters!"

"Quit your complaining, Symington. You have to take to the boats like the rest of the crew," Mr. Allan said.

"I'm a bloody carpenter!" Symington growled. "I should get blisters doing my work, not yours!"

Christopher jumped in. "What is the captain to do? He has a reputation to keep."

"Then let *'im* man the boats! Maybe the captain has forgotten 'oo 'e really is."

"Enough, Symington," Mr. Allan said. "Do not disrespect the captain!"

It was Smitty, not Mr. Allan, who silenced Symington's complaints. Smitty whispered in the carpenter's ear.

Hiding in the passageway, Annie felt chills run down her spine as she watched Symington slowly nod his head, a sinister grin on his face. Smitty whispered to yet another sailor, then another. Except for the creaking and groaning of the ship, all was quiet. Annie relaxed once the whispering ceased and the playing cards were dealt.

While her arms ached from the day's rowing, Annie sat back listening to the off-key songs and tall tales. She patiently waited to hear Samuel Baggott's tenor voice. But no sooner had he begun to sing, Smitty and Symington rushed out of the fo'c'sle. Annie jumped to her feet, but it was too late. Trapped between the two sailors, she had nowhere to escape.

"What have we here?" Smitty gripped Annie around her neck, his boney fingers digging into her flesh. "Why don't you join us, lad?"

"Be our guest." Symington sneered.

"I need to get back to Doc's cabin." She pulled away from Smitty's grasp, only to have him grab her upper arm.

"But we do mind. You hurt our feelings turnin' down our invitation," Smitty said. As if he were genuinely offended, his lower lip curled up. He then threw back his head and laughed.

Symington scoffed. "Ain't we good enough for ye, boy?"

Stooping to avoid the low overhead, Smitty shoved Annie into the fo'c'sle while Symington walked unobstructed. Sailors rolled out of hammocks, others stood up from their cards. All crowded closer.

Penned in, Annie gasped in the moist fetid air. She searched for a friendly face. The amicable Mr. Allan was nowhere to be found, but she saw Barrette. Since he had been a prisoner of the press gang, Annie believed he would understand her plight, but he avoided her gaze.

Seeing Christopher through a gap in the throng, Annie's spirits buoyed, but were quickly dashed. He, too, ignored her plight while he whittled a piece of wood with frenzied abandon.

Smitty pulled his sea chest out from under his hammock. "Have a seat, Andrés."

Annie's legs went limp before Smitty pushed her down onto his sea chest.

Symington bent down and hissed in her ear, "My little maggot, do ye know what we do to spies?"

CHAPTER TWENTY-THREE

Defiant, Annie attempted to stand but Smitty shoved her back down.

"Spy? Who would I be spying for?"

"The captain, to tell him about our gamblin'."

"I wouldn't do that."

"Oh, wouldn't ye, now," Symington said. "Ye never liked me, much. Don't deny it"

"Half the crew doesn't like you, Symington." Annie looked around at the stunned faces staring back at her. "It's the truth," she said. "But I hold no grudge against any of you."

"Don't believe 'im," Symington said.

"Bet you told the captain about our fightin', too," Smitty said.

She had never seen any fighting. Pushing and shoving, maybe, but no real fighting. Some spy I am, she thought.

"Close yer eyes, boy!" Symington ordered.

"Wha—what?" Beads of perspiration soaked through Annie's shirt.

"Are ye deaf? Close yer eyes!"

She gawked at Symington and played her last card. "I don't have to do anything you tell me to do. I am Captain Hawke's cabin boy."

In a high pitch voice, Smitty repeated her words, "I am Captain Hawke's cabin boy."

The men broke out in laughter. Her heart sunk wondering if Christopher and Barrette had joined in.

Symington raised his hand to hush the rowdy crowd. He surveyed the fo'c'sle with jaundiced eyes. "Ye think being Cap'n 'awke's cabin boy means anything down 'ere?"

Courage drained from Annie's voice. "Aye?"

"Captain 'awke doesn't set foot in 'ere and we're not guests in 'is cabin. What goes on down 'ere is none o 'is business. And we want to keep it that way. Now, do as yer told. Close yer eyes, maggot."

Slouched over, she closed her eyes so tight they hurt. Water lapping against the ship's hull contrasted sharply with the blood Annie heard surging in her ears.

"Let's throw him overboard," Smitty said.

"Too quick. I say we keelhaul 'im. If yer lucky, my little maggot, ye will drown before the barnacles on the bottom of the ship rip ye to pieces," Symington said. "Ye might even survive, but I guess ye'd be missing a limb or two. We will be real quiet while ye make up yer mind."

Annie shook her head. This can't be happening, she thought, but she wasn't giving up. Annie opened her eyes and stared Symington in the face. "You will never get away with this."

"The more I think about it, throwing you overboard is the best idea," Symington said. "Sailors fall overboard all the time. The cap'n will think it was just a terrible accident. Now, close yer eyes or I'll close them for ye."

The fo'c'sle became deathly silent once more. Her eyes shut tight, Annie waited—and wondered. Why did she have to keep her eyes closed? Why didn't Symington and his cohorts simply get the ugly deed over with? Was it to torture her? That must be it, she thought, and they were doing a grand job of it.

When she thought she could no longer endure the wait, she heard two sets of footsteps coming toward her. She stiffened, but could tell it wasn't Symington or Smitty. One pair of footsteps was uneven, the other, strong and confident. Christopher? Barrette?

"Andrés, open your eyes."

Annie trusted no one, not even Christopher. Besides, if he had come to her rescue, he did not stand a chance against her shipmates, now her enemies.

Christopher's request turned into a chant. One by one, the sailors joined in. "Open your eyes!"

The chorus grew more insistent to a full crescendo. "Open your eyes! Open your eyes!"

Close your eyes. Open your eyes. Why can't they make up their minds? Like the tears she choked back when her family died, Annie refused to succumb to the scream building in her throat. She then felt a warm breath on the nape of her neck.

"Open your eyes, Andrés. I promise no one will harm you."

First Christopher, now Barrette, Annie relaxed her

shoulders. Maybe she was to receive a stay of execution. She was in no great hurry to find out. Afraid of what she might see, Annie took her time opening her eyes.

Several feet in front of her, Christopher and Barrette stood on either side of Mr. Allan. They looked at her sympathetically, while Mr. Allan's cheery grin caught Annie completely off guard.

"Don't be frightened, lad," he told her.

Only seconds before, she was to meet a horrible death. Now she was told not to be frightened. She wondered if she were going mad.

Her gaze fell to the bosun's hands. He held out a knife belt. A carved ivory monkey peeked above its leather sheath.

"Do you remember this?" he asked.

Annie's head bobbed up and down. "It is Captain Hawke's lucky knife."

"Wasn't lucky for old Mason Rain," muttered Smitty.

"It is *your* knife, Andrés, the one the captain promised you." Mr. Allan said. "He knew you couldn't have a blade as fine as this one without a proper knife belt."

He motioned for her to stand. Her legs still wobbly, Annie complied.

Symington thumped her on the back of the head. "Scared ye spitless, didn't we?"

Wanting so badly to punch him, Annie balled her hands into fists, but she restrained herself.

Mr. Allan motioned for Annie to raise her arms as he wrapped the belt around her slender waist. He admired his handiwork. "Ah, a splendid fit."

The crew burst into cheers of, "Huzzah!"

"It is quite handsome, sir." Confused, she scanned the faces of what now appeared to be friendly shipmates. "I don't understand what just happened."

Mr. Allan explained. "Nothing gets past the captain. He told me to give it to you during one of your nightly visits."

"Yer spying," said Symington.

Annie got in his face. "No—my *visits*, that's what Captain Hawke called them."

Mr. Allan chuckled. "The men needed something to amuse themselves, been some long days."

Annie thought a moment. "So, I was nothing more than the crew's entertainment for the evening. Well, I hope I satisfied you."

Annie glared at the men. Some looked away while others shuffled their feet. "Maybe next time you could simply ask me to sing a song or dance a jig for you. Oh, I know something even better. Maybe you could ask me to punch Symington in the face. Now, that would be entertaining."

"I would like to see ye try," Symington said.

"Now, now, we don't want to have any hard feelings," Mr. Allan said as he wedged himself between Annie and Symington. "You do know, Andrés, you are always welcome here in the fo'c'sle. Why don't you find yourself a hammock?"

Barrette broke in, "Mr. Allan, if I had a choice to sleep in the surgeon's cabin or in the fo'c'sle with a bunch of sweaty tars, I know which one I would choose."

Barrette to the rescue, again, Annie thought.

"A point well taken, Barrette." Mr. Allan slapped Annie on the back, almost knocking her off her feet. "Off with you, now, Andrés."

The sailors made a path for Annie as she made her way to the passageway. Symington's parting words resounded in her ears. "Scared 'im so bad, I am surprised the little maggot's 'eart is still beating."

* * *

Annie felt her way through the darkened cabin to where her blankets should have been. She patted the deck. They weren't there. Slightly lifting her head, Annie's forehead bumped into what felt like canvas.

A candle sputtered to life in Doc's hand. "Do you like it?"

"Oh, my!" Annie faced a hammock just her size. "Is it mine?"

"It certainly is."

She quickly removed the knife belt, placed it on the desk and pulled herself into the canvas. "Doc, it is perfect. Thank you so much."

"Don't thank me. Captain Hawke had Baggot and Carter set it up."

"The captain always expected me to move into the fo'c'sle. Now I have a hammock and we both know what that means. This is permanent, Doc. I get to stay here. But I don't understand. The captain had been so adamant about me moving into the fo'c'sle."

"Apparently, he changed his mind."

"Just like that," Annie snapped her fingers. "There must be a reason."

"The important thing is you can stay here with me."

Annie took off her cap and tossed it on the table. "Did you know I had been going to the fo'c'sle at night?"

"Yes, Captain Hawke informed me. You are a spirited one, just like my Emily was. Now go to sleep."

"Doc…"

"Whatever it is, it can wait until tomorrow—too much excitement for one night."

As Doc extinguished the light, Annie ran her fingers through her damp hair. "I have the forenoon watch tomorrow."

"No more talking. Good night," Doc said.

Annie remembered something Symington had said that troubled her. "Earlier this evening, Doc, Symington said something about the captain forgetting who he really is. Do you know what he meant by that?"

"No, I don't, and I suggest you don't worry about it. Now, go to sleep."

Annie knew it would be fruitless to pursue the subject further. "Good night, Doc," Annie said as the hammock hugged her into a contented sleep.

CHAPTER TWENTY-FOUR

Annie woke to the sound of eight bells. She poured herself out of the hammock. "That was the best sleep I have ever had."

"Last night, did you say something about the forenoon watch?" Doc said as he stirred his tea.

"Uh huh."

"Well, if you have the forenoon watch, you are late. The morning watch just ended."

"Just ended! I thought it just started. How could you have let me sleep in?"

"You looked so peaceful. I did not wish to wake you," Doc said between sips of tea. "Don't worry. You won't be flogged for not bringing the captain his breakfast."

"It is not his breakfast I am worried about. I am to be a lookout today, or at least I was supposed to be. Do you have any idea how important that is? This might be my last chance to prove that I am a sailor."

Annie grabbed her cap off the table, and then slung the knife belt over her shoulder as she bounded for the door.

"Stow your hammock," Doc called after her.

"No time!" Annie said as she ran out of the cabin.

* * *

As Annie poked her head through the opened hatch, Captain Hawke waved his hand in the air. "Look men, Mr. de la Cruz has decided to join us this fine morning."

There goes that eyebrow again, Annie thought as she climbed out onto the deck. She finished buckling her belt.

"Take Christopher's place. Now!"

"Aye, aye, Captain."

Relieved she was still going to be a lookout, she made her way up the shrouds with the spyglass tucked in at her waist. Annie passed Christopher on his way down. "Good luck, mate," he said.

Annie gave him a weak smile.

* * *

Two bells sounded. It was an hour into the forenoon watch. With the wind stinging her cheeks and the sails snapping below her, Annie scanned the sea with her spyglass.

Four bells. Perched high on the lookout platform, she watched a whale breach the surface before plunging below the sea. "It is amazing up here."

Six bells. She saw no more whales. The ocean stretched endlessly in every direction. Whether she shifted her weight from one foot to the other, her legs cramped.

Seven bells sounded. For what seemed like the hundredth time, Annie lifted her arm. With the spyglass to her eye, she saw a smattering of clouds on the horizon. Then she saw it, a two-masted ship. She admired it a moment then moved the glass lower. She saw yet another vessel. Annie studied this one longer than the first.

Annie's heart pounded. "Two ships off to larboard. One is listing on her starboard side. The foremast and mainmast are down. There is another ship, a brigantine!" Annie shouted.

Captain Hawke summoned Perry. He sent the sailor aloft to verify Annie's sighting.

After climbing the shrouds, Perry stood next to Annie and gazed through the glass.

"Do you see it?" Annie asked.

"Our eyes often play tricks on us when we are out at sea, Andrés" he said.

"I didn't imagine it, Perry, if that is what you are implying. I know I saw two ships."

Perry continued searching. "Well, I'll be," he said. "Captain! Two ships. One's adrift."

"Is one a brigantine?"

"Aye, Captain!"

"Perry, hand Andrés the glass."

Annie peered through it again.

"The two ships, what are their colors?" the Captain shouted.

"Can't see either of their colors, Captain," Annie yelled back. "But the brigantine's coming about."

Annie waited. It seemed like an eternity. Then she saw it. "Skull and crossbones! She's a bloody pirate ship!"

CHAPTER TWENTY-FIVE

"All hands on deck!" The captain roared, "Mr. Montgomery, assemble a boarding party."

The Realm changed course.

Annie handed the glass back to Perry and scrambled down the ratlines. She wasn't about to miss any opportunity that would put her in the good graces of her shipmates. She needed to be in that boarding party.

No sooner had she landed on the deck, Captain Hawke stopped her.

"Tell me about the ship in full sail," he said.

Not being able to think of anything more to tell him, she instead asked, "The brigantine, Captain, could she be..." Annie knew if ever there was a time to mention the unmentionable, this was it. "Could she be the Crimson Revenge?"

Captain Hawke's eyes narrowed, but not at her. He looked in the direction of the two ships. "A distinct possibility."

"Then shouldn't we be heading away from her and not toward her?"

"We are heading to the crippled vessel, not the pirate ship, Andrés. That one will be long gone before we get there. You are dismissed."

Now that was a waste of time, Annie thought, as she dashed off to find Mr. Montgomery assembling his men for the boarding party.

"I want to be in the boarding party, sir," she said.

"Sorry, lad, I have already chosen my men."

"I spotted the ship, sir. It seems only fitting that I should board her."

Mr. Montgomery mulled it over and said, "Only because you're the one who spotted the ship, Andrés, will I ask the men if any of them are willing to give up their place for you. But don't get your hopes up."

"Sir, Andrés can take my place on the boarding party." Barrette offered.

Mr. Montgomery looked from Barrette to Annie. "Very well then, Andrés, you can take Barrette's place. This is serious business. You will follow orders. Is that understood?"

"Aye, sir."

"If the ship hasn't sunk by the time we get there, you are paired with me."

* * *

When the Realm came a safe distance alongside the drifting ship, the longboat was lowered into the sea.

Mr. Montgomery commanded, "Man the boat!"

As the sailors clambered aboard, Annie looked around at the crew. Seeing their grim faces, she wondered if she had made the right decision.

Once the men pushed off, head oarsman Ainsworth, ordered, "Together, pull!"

While the oars sliced through the sea, salt water

sprayed Annie's face. With each stroke, the gap narrowed between the two ships.

"Andrés, pick up the stroke!"

Annie pulled harder. She glanced over her shoulder. Not anchored, the ship's position had changed. She saw painted on the stern in bold letters its name, the Margaret Louise.

Approaching the starboard side, Mr. Montgomery shouted, "Ahoy!" He waited, but only the groans of a dying ship greeted him.

After he hurled a grappling hook over the ship's railing, Mr. Montgomery put his full weight on the rope. Confident the line was secure, he sent Rodrigues up the side while Ainsworth and his oarsmen kept the boat steady. It took Rodrigues no time to scale the side of the ship. As soon as he was aboard, he disappeared from view. When he reappeared, he held the Margaret Louise's rope ladder in his hands.

Mr. Montgomery shouted, "Any survivors?"

Dropping the ladder over the side, Rodrigues yelled down, "I saw only one sailor and he's dead, looks about Christopher's age."

Despite the chill in the air, Annie wiped sweat from her palms onto her trousers. She looked over at Christopher. All color had drained from his face.

Mr. Montgomery ordered the rest of the boarding party up the side. Annie nervously waited her turn as she watched each sailor ascend the ladder. Her turn came all too soon. Annie gripped the ladder, inhaled deeply, and began her climb.

"Steady as you go," Mr. Montgomery said.

Making her way up, Annie climbed over the railing. She joined the sailors assembled at one of the fallen masts staring down at the crushed body of a sailor. Christopher nudged it with his foot.

"What you expect him to do, mate, get up and dance a jig for you?" Baggott said

"Saints preserve me," Carter whispered while Rodrigues made the sign of the cross.

Mr. Montgomery climbed over the railing. Everyone stepped aside for him to inspect the sailor who looked up with unseeing eyes. Observing that the man was obviously dead, Mr. Montgomery was more concerned with the sharp angle of the deck.

"We don't have much time. Carter, Baggott check the storage areas. Christopher, Rodrigues stay on the upper deck and check under the downed canvass for any sailors who might have survived and are hiding. Andrés and I will make a quick sweep of the fo'c'sle and the quarters below."

"Shouldn't there be blood on the deck?" Christopher asked.

"A sudden squall must have washed it away," Mr. Montgomery replied.

Annie and her shipmates cautiously climbed over what had once been proud masts, now nothing more than splintered wood and canvass. Making their way to the hatch, she and Mr. Montgomery avoided the gaping holes in the deck.

* * *

Where men had once shared tall tales and laughter, the fo'c'sle stood in stark disorder. Mr. Montgomery pushed aside an empty sea chest.

"Where are the bodies?" she asked.

"I suspect they were thrown overboard."

Annie searched under blankets and stowed hammocks, hoping to find someone, anyone, alive. "Maybe they escaped," Annie said.

"No, the boats are still lashed to the deck."

"I didn't see any bodies floating in the water."

"Sharks," Mr. Montgomery replied. "But if it is Godenot's work, don't expect to find any bodies. This is now a ghost ship. Those not thrown overboard became his prisoners to torture or to become members of his crew."

"I would kill myself before I would become one of his pirates."

"Don't judge," Mr. Montgomery said.

Annie skirted around smeared blood, only to have broken glass pierce her bare foot. She grimaced in pain as she pulled out the jagged shard.

"I'll search aft. You go forward," Mr. Montgomery said.

Annie heard noises coming from the far end of the passageway. "A very large rat," Annie said. "But just in case…" She shifted the candlestick to her left hand and drew out her knife to investigate.

With the increased listing of the ship, it became more difficult to stand upright. Annie slid to the door to what she believed was the first mate's quarters.

Annie saw a sliver of light under it. As soon as she pushed the handle down with her elbow, the door flew open.

Overturned chairs had shifted to one side of the cabin. The furniture obscured her view, but not enough to hide a figure cowering against the bulkhead, knees drawn to his chest. The smell of urine invaded her senses.

"I won't harm..." A flash and a thunderous blast ended Annie's sentence. The candle and knife flew out of her hands.

Annie groped for the knife lying inches from her fingertips, but the searing pain in her right arm wouldn't let her grab it. She realized the unthinkable. "I been shot!"

In the glow of the lantern hanging overhead, the shooter clutched a pistol with both hands. He shook so badly, she thought it was only luck that he had hit her.

He looked to be about ten years old. The boy sobbed. "Don't kill me."

To Annie's relief, he made no effort to prime the pistol again with powder and shot. As she pressed the wound with her hand, blood oozed between her fingers. Her teeth chattered. "I won't kill you," she said. "Why did you shoot me?"

"You're a pirate."

"A p-pirate?" Her eyes darted from the boy to her injured arm and back again. "Do I look like a pirate?" She fought to stay alert. "I am a ca-cabin boy, just l-like you."

No longer speaking in a hushed tone, the boy sat up straight. "I'm not a cabin boy. I am David Palmer, son of Captain Harold Palmer, commander of this ship."

"P-pleased t-to meet...." Annie's world went black.

CHAPTER TWENTY-SIX

The moment Mr. Montgomery burst into the cabin, Annie's eyes fluttered open. Immediately he put himself between her and the boy. He raised his pistol, the boy in his sights. "Put your weapon down!" he shouted.

Palmer crossed his hands over his face. "Don't shoot!" But the pistol remained in his hand.

Mr. Montgomery shoved aside a chair with his foot before snatching the empty weapon from the boy. He tossed it in the corner while shoving his own pistol into his waistband.

With the boy disarmed, Mr. Montgomery turned his full attention to Annie. He dropped to one knee. "That's a nasty wound, lad."

Nestled in the crook of Mr. Montgomery's arm, Annie squinted up into his face. Like a drunken sailor who had imbibed too long at the Black Anchor Pub, she asked in all seriousness, "Why is there t-two of you?"

"Maybe, because one of me is not enough to take care of you," Mr. Montgomery said.

Annie attempted to laugh, but the pain turned it into a groan.

Hoping to stop the bleeding, Mr. Montgomery

quickly ripped off a strip of material from his sleeve and wrapped the makeshift bandage around Annie's arm. She pursed her lips together while the red circle grew larger on the cloth. As she drifted in and out of consciousness, she told Mr. Montgomery what had occurred.

Mr. Montgomery steadied himself on the slanting deck. He bent down, picked up Annie, and tossed her over his shoulder. To Palmer, he commanded, "On your feet, boy, to the hatch!"

* * *

Annie woke cradled in Mr. Montgomery's arms as the first mate slid to the railing. She expected to see the Crimson Revenge looming over the side, but Captain Hawke was right. The pirate ship was nowhere to be seen.

Palmer climbed down the rope ladder. With no time left to climb down himself, Mr. Montgomery dropped Annie over the side. Christopher leaped across Carter's lap, catching her as she fell through the air. "You're bleeding," he said before he leaned her up against Palmer.

Ainsworth and Rodrigues dove out of the way, as Mr. Montgomery came crashing near the bow of the longboat. Under Ainsworth's skillful guidance,the oarsmen kept the boat from capsizing.

"Shove off!" Ainsworth shouted.

"Together! Pull smartly!"

"Steady!"

The boat crew briskly rowed until Ainsworth

yelled, "That is well!"

Safely away from the sinking ship, the sailors watched the Margaret Louise in her final death throes. Shrouded in a grey mist, she groaned one last time before rolling all the way onto her starboard side. The sound of cracking timber filled the air as the ocean boiled over the Margaret Louise. While the ship descended to her watery grave, Palmer clutched Annie's hand, his nails digging into her flesh.

CHAPTER TWENTY-SEVEN

"Boat your oars!"

The men passed the oars overhead, stacking them down the center, blades toward the bow. Barrette and Perry hauled Annie up to the deck in an improvised sling. Once she was safely on the deck, Barrette held her limp body, supporting her head with his hand.

"Make way!" commanded Captain Hawke.

"Careful!" Doc cautioned.

The men craned their necks as Barrette laid her on the deck. Doc came prepared for all emergencies with his small cabinet full of medicine and equipment. He quickly removed the strip of fabric wound tightly around Annie's arm to examine the wound.

"Is the little maggot goin' to live?" Symington asked.

Thinking she had heard genuine concern in the carpenter's voice, Annie assumed she must surely be delirious.

"Andrés will live. The ball went clear through the arm," Doc said. He took out a bottle of an astringent and rubbed it into the wound to slow the bleeding.

Mr. Allan piped orders, dispersing the men to their stations.

Doc prepared to sew Annie's arm, first giving her

laudanum for the pain.

Captain Hawke knelt beside her. "How's the arm, boy?"

Annie gritted her teeth. "H-hurts."

"Who shot you?"

Annie took hold of the captain's sleeve. "Not his fault."

"Not whose fault?" he said.

"No more questions. He needs his strength," Doc said.

Captain Hawke stood and scanned the deck. "Who, the bloody hell, shot my cabin boy?"

Mr. Montgomery nodded toward Christopher who was trying to calm Palmer down.

"Him?" the captain said. "He is a mere child."

"He mistook Andrés for a pirate," Mr. Montgomery said.

"Is he blind?" Captain Hawke said.

"From what Andrés was able to tell me, the lad saw his knife. Thinking Andrés was a pirate, he shot him."

Christopher spoke up while the boy cursed at him, "He believes we are all pirates."

Palmer clamped his teeth down on Christopher's hand. Christopher's immediate reaction was to let the boy go. Palmer made a break for it, running for the railing. Before he could jump over the side of the ship, Captain Hawke grabbed the boy and whipped him around. Palmer tried to pull away while kicking out at the captain, but Captain Hawke wouldn't loosen his hold.

CHAPTER TWENTY-EIGHT

The captain clasped one of the ropes securing Annie's hammock to the overhead. "You look better than you did yesterday, boy," he said.

"I am as fit as a fiddle, Captain," Annie replied.

"Don't listen to him," Doc said. "He needs more than a day to heal."

Annie tried to raise her head, but the captain touched her shoulder. "Not so fast."

The captain then took Annie's arm in his hand to get a closer look at her stitches. "Nice work, Doc."

Annie moaned. "Mason Rain's monkey knife wasn't very lucky, Captain."

"You are alive, aren't you? And if it had hit the bone, you might have lost your arm. Sounds like you were very lucky," he said with a smile.

"I am lucky only because Palmer is such a bad shot," Annie said.

Captain Hawke looked at Doc. "How soon will the boy be up and about?"

"I won't know for a few days," Doc said. "But barring infection, the lad should make a full recovery. For now, he needs plenty of rest."

"All you have to do, Andrés, is lie here and not work. I think your shipmates would like some of your luck."

Annie frowned. "I would rather be working than shot, Captain. How is Palmer?"

"He insists he be treated like the rest of the crew. He will pay you a visit this afternoon." Captain Hawke folded his arms across his chest. "Alright Andrés, I can see something is bothering you. Out with it."

"Why didn't we go after the pirate ship?"

"In case you haven't noticed, this is a merchant ship, not a warship."

"Then why have all those cannons if we aren't going to use them," Annie said.

"We have all those cannons so if we are attacked, we can fight back," The captain replied. "Did you not learn anything from being on the Margaret Louise? I will never risk my men's lives unless it is absolutely necessary. My decks will not become slippery with my crew's blood if I can help it." Captain Hawke said as he stomped out of the cabin.

* * *

After three days of recuperation, the captain's outburst was nothing more than a hazy memory. Full movement returned to Annie's arm, but not without pain. Enjoying the concern shown by her shipmates, she wasn't anxious to resume her duties.

Christopher chuckled as he walked into Doc's cabin. He held a book in the air. "Another one, Andrés." He tossed the book with the others before pulling up a chair.

"I don't wish to hurt the captain's feelings, but I

cannot possibly read them all," Annie said.

Pounding on the door interrupted their conversation.

"It must be Barrette," Annie said. "He knocks on the door as if he were hammering on an anvil."

Christopher looked around the room. "Doc needs more chairs."

Barrette sauntered into the cabin balancing Annie's dinner tray in one hand. "It should be me lying there, not you. I never should have given up my place on the boarding party."

"You're jealous," Christopher said.

"Why would I be jealous?" Barrette said.

"Andrés will have a battle scar and you won't."

"Ah, you found me out, Christopher." Barrette grinned as he set the tray in front of Annie.

"Did you know Palmer paid me a visit? He apologized for shooting me...again." Annie said.

"Well, that is mighty big of him, considering the captain should have keel-hauled the boy or at the very least flogged him for what he did to you," Barrette said.

"The captain knows Palmer mistook me for a pirate."

"How could anyone mistake *you* for a pirate?"

"Have some sympathy for the boy. After all, he lost his father," Annie said.

"I have more sympathy for him than Symington does. He blames Palmer for everything." Barrette cleared his throat. "That boy is a bad one. Why is it 'e survived and no one else did? Lucky for 'im. Unlucky for them. 'E's a Jonah, that one is."

Christopher cocked his head. "I am impressed, mate. You sounded just like the old tar."

"You two had better keep an eye on Palmer, Annie said. "I don't want to hear he has fallen overboard if you know what I mean."

The door suddenly opened. "I hate to break up this little tea party," Doc said. "But unless you have been shot, you do not belong here."

"Get better, Andrés," Christopher said as he headed for the door.

"Thanks, Christopher," Annie said. "And by the way Barrette, that was your best imitation of Symington yet."

Barrette bowed to her while backing out the door. He was barely in the passageway when Doc slammed the door in his face

"That was rude," Annie said.

Doc mumbled something unintelligible.

Annie sighed. "Doc, have you ever noticed Barrette's dimples?"

She pressed her fingers into both cheeks.

"No, I have not noticed his dimples and neither should you," Doc said shaking his finger at her. "You are a young lady who should not be entertaining young men alone, especially that Barrette fellow."

"You can't be serious. He doesn't know I'm a girl. So what difference does it make?"

"Don't be so sure about that," Doc said.

"What's that supposed to mean?"

"I don't like the way he acts around you."

"You are suspicious by nature, Doc. Besides, Captain Hawke said I needed to earn the respect of the men and I have done just that." She grimaced in pain as she raised her stitched arm in the air. "I've earned their respect as well as Barrette's, and he shows me nothing more." She murmured under her breath, "Unfortunately."

"I heard that," Doc said. "No matter, soon he and the rest of the men will have more important things on their minds."

"What could possibly be more important than this?" She raised her arm again.

"Landing in the American colonies," Doc said.

Annie had only a moment to think what that meant for her when a lilting melody drifted into the cabin. "Is that Samuel Baggott?"

"That it is. The captain told him how much you enjoy his singing," Doc said.

"Ah, that was nice of him." Odd, she thought, but nice.

Annie let out a light breath and closed her eyes. She escaped to a world of chamber orchestras where fine ladies dress in elaborate gowns and gentlemen wear fancy waistcoats and buckled shoes.

By the fifth day, Christopher, not Barrette, brought Annie her meals and the stack of books grew no taller. It was time to return to her duties.

CHAPTER TWENTY-NINE

As each day passed, the more anxious Annie became. The thought of leaving the Realm for even a moment made her uneasy.

"Doc, I will never leave the Realm." Annie waited for his reply. "Say something?"

"What do you want me to say, that I am glad you will become like me? I would not wish my life on anyone."

"But you have a good life here, Doc."

"While you have made my life more bearable, this is not living. Hidden away in the bowels of a ship is no life, Annie, not for me and not for you."

"Dry land has not been kind to me, Doc. You, of all people, should understand that better than anyone."

He shook his head. "Being on the land or the sea has nothing to do with heartache. Granted, my saddest days were on land, but so were my happiest."

* * *

As the Realm sailed into Charles Town's harbor, Annie admired the buildings dotting the waterfront. Some were as high as three stories. Colorful potted plants adorned balconies where girls waved to the sailors who eagerly waved back. Nothing she saw changed her mind about leaving the Realm.

Annie hadn't gone ashore in Boston or Philadelphia, but she feared Charles Town would be a different matter. It was the Realm's last port o' call. She knew all too well that if Captain Hawke ordered her off the ship, she would have to go.

* * *

"Come along, Andrés," Mr. Montgomery said.

"Do I have a choice?" Annie said as she joined him at the end of the gangway.

"When Captain Hawke gives an order, that is the end of it."

Annie walked beside him. "The men told me about their time in Boston and Philadelphia. What they did there was no different from what they do in London, get drunk and fight. Is that what the captain expects me to do?"

"Enough, Andrés."

"Land has not been..." Annie knew it was of little use to finish the sentence. She had grown tired of her own lament, as had Captain Hawke. It undoubtedly would have little effect on Mr. Montgomery.

Walking past the courthouse and deeper into town, she decided a new tactic might work. "There certainly are a lot of things to see and do here, sir."

"That is quite true."

Pretending she was interested, she peered into shops and the music houses where sailors could dance and be entertained for a price. As they approached the town square, she observed young women twirling their parasols talking to well-dressed gentlemen.

Annie stopped. "My, my, will you look at that. If you didn't have to drag me around town, sir, a handsome man such as yourself, would have no problem meeting one of those fine looking women."

Mr. Montgomery sighed. "Meeting women has never been my problem. Finding one to my liking, however, has."

"And what is to your liking, sir? Red hair, black..."

"It has nothing to do with hair, Andrés. Finding one who is beautiful, intelligent, and tall is not so simple, especially the tall part. Did I mention beautiful?"

"Twice," Annie said. "How tall are we talking about, sir?"

"I want to gaze into her eyes, not the top of a silly bonnet."

"Too bad Abigail isn't here," Annie murmured.

Mr. Montgomery stroked his clean-shaven chin. "Is there something you would care to tell me about you and this damsel?"

"Me and—and Abigail?" Annie stammered while her face turned a bright red. "Oh no, you have it all wrong. All I meant to say was that she is tall."

Mr. Montgomery burst out in laughter. When he finally could talk, he knocked Annie playfully in the shoulder. "I am only teasing you, lad."

Annie took a deep breath. "Like I was saying, Mr. Montgomery, you will meet no fine ladies, tall, short or otherwise, if you have me with you."

"A point well taken," he said. "But we cannot go

against the captain's orders."

Annie kicked at a pebble on the ground. "It was worth a try."

"I am not happy about this arrangement either, Andrés. If you must know, I suggested you go into town with Christopher and Barrette, but Captain Hawke said Barrette would probably get you into all kinds of trouble."

"He was probably right about that," Annie said.

"Neither of us has a choice in this matter, so we might as well make the best of it. Besides, the captain wanted me to teach you some of the history of Charles Town."

"Not only did he make me leave the Realm, he wants you to bore me to death."

"He said you are a curious young man. It would be a part of your education." Mr. Montgomery continued, "Did you know that Charles Town prides itself in its religious tolerance?"

"And did you know that Blackbeard sailed into Charles Town with four of his ships, kidnapped some of its citizens and held them for ransom? I believe that was in 1718," Annie said.

Abigail used to tease Annie about all the useless information floating around in her head. Maybe, that same useless information would now benefit her, she thought.

"To be quite frank, lad, I do not believe the captain cared if you learned about the town's history or not. He wanted you off the ship, plain and simple, and with someone who would keep you safe."

"I didn't know he cared," Annie said sarcastically.

"Hmm" Mr. Montgomery appeared lost in thought.

"What are you thinking?" Annie asked.

"The captain never said how long you had to be off the ship."

"Are you thinking what I'm thinking?"

Mr. Montgomery smiled. "I believe I have fulfilled my part of the order. As far as I am concerned, you are free to return to the Realm."

Annie was about to bolt. "You mean now, this very second?"

"Not so fast, lad," Mr. Montgomery said. "The captain said not to let you out of my sight. We will head back to the ship together. Once you are safely on the Realm, I can then enjoy myself in Charles Town."

"I must admit, Mr. Montgomery, it was a pleasure spending what little time I had in Charles Town with you, but it will take an act of God before I ever set foot on dry land again."

CHAPTER THIRTY

Sailors prepared the Realm for her journey back to England. Provisions were replenished and the cargo hold filled with deerskins, rice, timber and barrels of indigo. Aft of the cannons, where chickens roosted in their cages, Christopher herded pigs into a pen.

"Thanks for helping, Andrés."

Annie cuddled a lamb in her arms. "I am sorry you did most of the work, Christopher, but have you ever seen anything so cute?"

"Don't get too attached. His days are numbered."

Annie covered the lamb's ears. "You didn't hear that, Wooly"

"Now don't go naming the captain's dinner, Andrés."

* * *

On the quarterdeck, Annie looked up into the scarlet sky, beautiful, yet ominous all at the same time. "It's going to be a bad one," Annie said.

"Red sky in morning, sailors take warning," Christopher said.

The wind picked up as lightening flashed across the grey sky. Sails were shortened, cargo and water casks secured. By early afternoon, the morning drizzle had turned into a downpour. Waves surged over the bow and seawater seeped into the passageways.

Captain Hawke shouted above the deafening roar of the storm, "Andrés, Palmer go below and assist Doc."

Annie believed her greatest challenge would be steadying patients while Doc set broken bones. She was wrong.

Four bells into the afternoon watch, the ship pitched violently sending Annie and Palmer to their knees. Doc braced himself against the bookshelf. He looked up at the overhead. Doc said under his breath, "It is going to be bad."

Annie and Palmer looked at each other. They both wondered what Doc knew that they didn't.

Doc's foreboding prediction proved true when Smitty stumbled into the cabin, his hand pressed firmly against his bleeding cheek. "Christopher's been hurt real bad, Doc. After Symington cuts him free, they will bring him down."

Annie twisted her shirt button. "Cut him free from what?"

Waiting for Doc to suture his cheek, Smitty only stared at Annie.

"What happened?!" Annie demanded.

"He can't talk now," Doc said as he did the first stitch.

After stitching up Smitty's cheek, Doc said, "The mast broke in two. Am I right?"

Smitty looked out the corner of his eye at a jagged scar running the length of his forearm. "The last time it happened, you sewed me up real good, Doc."

Annie could barely catch her breath. "This time, Smitty, what happened this time?"

"One of the sails unfurled. The wind caught it and the mizzenmast split in two just below the topgallant. That is when the yardarm went clear through him."

Annie refused to believe it. "You're lying!"

"I wish I was, Andrés."

"He's still alive?" Palmer whispered.

After what seemed like an eternity, Annie watched Perry and Rodrigues carry Christopher into the cabin. Nothing could have prepared her as she watched in horror at Barrette supporting Christopher's mid-section where Symington had neatly sawed off the yardarm. It jutted out several inches, front to back.

"On his side. Careful." Doc's voice didn't waver. "Steady."

If Annie didn't know any better, she would have thought Doc was directing something no more serious than a sprained ankle.

"Palmer, get a blanket. Andrés, the laudanum."

Doc's composed manner kept everyone calm except for Palmer. As Annie grabbed the painkiller from the cabinet, she turned in time to see Palmer turn white and fall backward. He grazed his head on the corner of the table before Smitty could catch him.

"Smitty, take Palmer out of here," Doc ordered.

Under Doc's instructions, Rodrigues, Perry and Barrette finished securing Christopher to the table.

Before leaving, Barrette brushed the hair from

Christopher's eyes. "You're in good hands, mate."

Barrette looked at Annie. He didn't say a word, only shook his head.

She stared back at him. "Just like Barrette said, Christopher, you're in good hands."

Barrette turned away and left.

"Christopher, does it hurt?" Doc asked.

"No, I feel...only cold." Fear clouded his blue eyes. "Am I going to die?"

"Sooner or later, we all die, son. We'll keep you comfortable." Doc took the bottle of laudanum from Annie's hands. "Andres, cover him with the blanket."

After Doc administered the painkiller, he put his flask to Christopher's mouth. The young sailor took only enough to wet his lips before he started coughing up blood.

Even with the blanket covering Christopher up to his neck, the image of the yardarm protruding from his body embedded itself in Annie's mind. She whispered to Doc, "Take it out."

He pulled her aside. "Even if I could, I would never be able to control the bleeding."

"Then what are you going to do?"

"Nothing."

Annie raised her voice. "You can't leave him like this. Do something."

Christopher gasped. "It's not so bad Andrés... really."

Annie came back to him and ran her trembling fingers through Christopher's hair. "Of course, it's not so bad. You are a fighter, Christopher, the bravest person I have ever known. Doc is going to fix you up. Tell him Doc."

Even if it was a lie, Annie needed to hear the words. "Tell him!"

"It's alright," Christopher mumbled.

"There must be something I can do for you, anything. Whatever it is, tell me," Annie said.

"Me mum, Andrés, promise me you will tell her I loved her."

"I promise, Christopher. But when I tell her, you will be standing right there beside me," Annie said.

She wanted to believe her own words, but she saw the truth in Christopher's eyes. Soon the boy who helped her become a sailor, her dearest friend, would be gone. Annie didn't know if she could live without him or if she even wanted to.

"I have one regret," Christopher said. "You won't tell anyone, will you? Don't want the crew laughin' at me."

"I won't tell a soul," Annie said.

"I never kissed a girl. Wanted to, but...too shy."

As his voice became weaker, Annie leaned closer. "Christopher, can you keep a secret?"

"To my grave," he answered with a cheerless grin.

"I am the daughter of a fisherman." Annie then pulled off her red cap and shook her head. Her black hair fell past her chin.

"I never kissed a boy," Annie whispered while she threaded her fingers through his hair.

Christopher's eyes widened. "You are...a girl?"

Annie continued to stroke his hair. "Shush now, Christopher. Just hold my hand."

His voice strained. "What is your name, milady?"

"Annie." The name caught in her throat. "Annie Moore."

"Kiss me, Annie Moore. After all, it is not like we don't know each other."

"With pleasure, my handsome Jack-tar."

Her lips touched his. When they parted, Christopher's hand tightened on hers. "Don't leave me," he said.

"I will never leave you."

His breathing labored, but his smile never left his chafed lips. Christopher closed his eyes.

Tears seared Annie's cheeks. "Christopher, don't you dare die on me!"

Doc put a mirror to his lips. It remained clear. "He's gone, Annie."

"I killed him."

"What are you talking about?"

"I'm cursed—just like Aunt Mary said I was."

Doc took Annie by the shoulders and shook her. "You had nothing to do with Christopher's death, or anyone's death. You are no more cursed than David Palmer is...than I am."

Annie passed her tongue across the bitter tears on her lips. As she buried her face in the blanket, she thought she heard the door open, but it didn't matter. Nothing mattered, not now, not ever again.

She felt a tender squeeze of her shoulder.

"A good cry will do you good, boy. It won't take away the pain, but it will ease it." The soothing words startled her.

She choked back a sob. "He can't be dead, Captain. He can't."

Captain Hawke let go of Annie's shoulder. She leaned back into the warmth of his chest. She watched as he drew the blanket over Christopher's face.

"No!" she cried. "Oh, please God, not Christopher, not my Christopher."

CHAPTER THIRTY-ONE

Only hours before, sailors fought to keep the Realm afloat. How unfair, Annie thought, as sunlight broke through the clouds where there was only a whisper of a breeze.

The shattered topgallant rested not far from where Annie assisted Smitty and Barrette in preparing Christopher for burial at sea. The usual joking Barrette didn't say a word as he tied a canvas bag onto his friend's body. The grief in his eyes reflected the ache in Annie's heart.

"What is in the bag?" Annie asked Smitty over the sound of pounding hummers and swishing saws.

"Cannon-shot," Smitty replied. "We want him to sink, you know."

Annie stiffened. She stared down at Christopher, his arms folded across his chest, his blond hair neatly combed.

Smitty smiled. "Christopher is the happiest looking corpse I ever saw."

While Annie sewed Christopher into his hammock, she agreed with Smitty. He did look happy, satisfied. Was it becaue of their kiss? Maybe, she thought, but she also knew Christopher had faced life with a happy disposition and an easy grin, so why not death.

Annie sewed the last stitch as carefully as the first.

The crew gathered round when the hammering and sawing stopped. Captain Hawke said a few words about the lad who had no enemies.

His eyes red and swollen, Mr. Allan read from Christopher's Bible. Its pages fell open to the 23rd Psalm, "Yea, though I walk through the valley of the shadow of death, I will fear no evil: for thou art with me ..."

After the bosun read the Bible passage, Captain Hawke looked at Annie. "Would you care to say a few words?"

Annie wanted to tell the crew what Christopher's friendship meant to her, how he made her laugh, how she admired him—how she wished he wasn't dead. But the words didn't come. "No," she said.

Mr. Montgomery recited the Lord's Prayer. A few members of the crew mumbled along with him while Christopher's body slid into the sea. Annie shuddered at its finality.

She expected the sailors to console each other or, at the very least, swap stories about Christopher, but the shrill blast on Mr. Allan's pipe made it clear—life aboard the Realm would go on like any other day. There was no time for grief or reflection. It was just as well. No words had comforted Annie when her family was laid to rest behind the stone church and none would comfort her now, she thought.

Once Symington's men repaired the damaged mast and the sails were mended, the Realm would continue her voyage back to England. Nothing changed. Yet, Annie knew everything had changed.

CHAPTER THIRTY-TWO

The next morning, Annie watched Samuel Baggot and Smitty carry Christopher's personal effects to the main deck while everyone assembled around the foremast.

An unused pipe, a deck of frayed playing cards were among the meager possessions auctioned off to the highest bidder.

With money Captain Hawke had given her, Annie placed it all on the last item up for bid.

"Five pounds," she called out.

No one bid against her. By the expressions on her shipmates' faces, they were pleased the sea chest went for more than the few shillings it was worth.

"Going once, going twice." Symington announced, "Sold! The little maggot is the proud owner of a mighty fine sea chest."

* * *

At the end of the second dog watch, Annie walked into Captain Hawke's cabin. "Mr. Montgomery said you wished to see me, Captain."

Not looking up, he waved his hand in the air. "I am almost finished, Andrés."

Annie peeked over his shoulder. She saw the words: *It was an honour to have known your son,* followed by the bold strokes of the captain's signature.

The captain rubbed his eyes as he brought the letter so close to his face that Annie wondered if it would touch his nose. He crinkled his brow.

"Are you all right, Captain?" Annie asked.

"Couldn't be better, boy."

Captain Hawke sealed the letter with wax. "This is for Christopher's mother. Once we drop anchor in England, you will accompany Mr. Montgomery to her home to pay your respects. Mr. Montgomery will then give Mrs. Doyle the letter and the proceeds from the auction." He hesitated. "I expected you to protest, Andrés—something about how 'dry land hasn't been kind to me' or some other sort of drivel."

"The sea hasn't been all that kind to me, either. Besides, I do want to meet Christopher's mum. I have a message for her from him."

"I know she will want to meet you." He smiled. "Doc told me you are telling a story in the fo'c'sle tonight."

"Aye, Captain."

"The men take their story telling seriously, Andrés. You will be going up against seasoned storytellers."

"I know, but they will really like my story."

* * *

Annie made her way into the fo'c'sle, squeezing in between Rodriques and Perry. Anxious for her turn, Annie paid little attention to Carter's story. Neither did his audience, which impatiently waited for Symington's turn.

Symington did not let the crew down. He told a lively tale of a shipwreck near a tropical island, where scantily clad women swam to their rescue. After his bawdy tale ended, it was Annie's turn.

"I wish to tell a story about a brave sailor."

Smitty asked, "What's it about?"

"I already told you, a brave sailor."

Ainsworth's muscles rippled across his bare chest. "Are there any mermaids in it?" he asked

Annie shook her head.

"How about sea monsters?"

Mr. Allan stood and quieted the men. "Let's hear it, Andrés."

Annie nervously tugged on her shirt button before beginning her tale. "One warm night..."

Symington grumbled. "Speak up. I can't 'ear ye, not that I want to."

Annie waited for the laughter to subside before she started again. "One warm night on a street in Port Royal, a handsome young sailor, Christopher was his name..."

She immediately had her audience's rapt attention.

Annie had to stop several times during her tale for her audience to oh and ah. It made little difference to the men that Christopher had never been to Port Royal or that he would surely run from a fight rather than be in the middle of one. The part where Christopher jumped between a fair maiden and six scoundrels, who had lust in their eyes and wickedness in their hearts, made the men cheer. But for Annie, all that mattered was that each new storyteller would embellish her tale of Christopher for years to come.

CHAPTER THIRTY-THREE

Annie woke with a start. It was always the same dream. Nothing she did could prevent Christopher's death.

She quickly lit the lantern. It wasn't only the dream she found disturbing. It was also the feelings her one kiss with Christopher had stirred inside her.

Annie ran her hands along her slim waist and fuller hips. The changes to her body confused her. Changes, so many changes, Annie thought

When she realized Doc was watching her, she blushed and tucked in her shirt.

He rolled out of his hammock. Without a word, he opened a drawer in his desk. He rummaged around until he brought out a tarnished sterling silver hairbrush. Several strands of golden hair clung to it. Doc tenderly wrapped the strands in a handkerchief before handing the monogrammed brush and matching mirror to Annie.

"I can't possibly use Emily's brush," Annie said.

"She would want you to," Doc said as he patted Annie's hand.

While Annie peered into the mirror, she studied every detail of her face, her slightly arched eyebrows. Her ice blue eyes contrasted with the red hue of her complexion, the color of the common sailor.

Annie brushed her hair behind her dainty ears. "Doc, do you think I am pretty?"

"You are just like my Emily, beautiful."

She put the mirror down and frowned.

"Is something wrong?" Doc asked.

"Why should I care? I'm a sailor."

"Only if you want to be."

Annie brought the mirror back to her face. Changes.

CHAPTER THIRTY-FOUR

The next evening, Annie gazed at her reflection in Emily's mirror. She then pulled her cap down to her eyebrows, pushing the dark strands of hair back under the cap and headed off to Captain Hawke's cabin.

She knocked, but got no answer. Annie shrugged and pushed the door open. No sooner had she entered to collect the captain's supper dishes, Annie ducked out of the way of a book flying toward her. It thudded against the door just above her head.

She picked up the book at her feet, wiped it on her shirt, and put it carefully on the shelf. "If this isn't a good time, Captain, I can come back later," Annie said as she looked about the book-strewn cabin.

"No, this is as good a time as any. Do you want them? I have no use for them."

Annie gathered two more books off the carpet. "But you love your books, Captain."

"They are old and mildewed," he replied.

She continued to shelve the books. "That never bothered you before."

The captain slouched in his chair. "It never bothered me before when I could see. There—I said it." He looked relieved with his confession.

Annie tiptoed across the rug. Inches from Captain

Hawke's face, she waved her hand in front of his eyes.

He cocked his head to the side, one eyebrow slightly raised. "What are you doing?"

Annie stumbled backward. "You said you couldn't see."

"I didn't say I was blind. I can't see the words in my books. My eyes have been going bad for some time now. It is almost too painful to read."

Without hesitating, Annie said, "I can read to you."

She watched him ponder the offer while he brushed his stubby black beard on the back of his knuckles.

Annie made the proposal more appealing. "If you *order* me to do it, Captain, then I must."

"Then an order, it is."

"When should I start, Captain?"

"Now."

While Annie perused his collection, Captain Hawke asked, "What are your plans when we drop anchor in England, boy?"

Annie pulled out a book, thumbed through its pages. "Except to visit Christopher's mum, I have no other plans."

"England's your home. There must be someone you wish to see?"

She put a book back and pulled out another. "Everyone I ever cared about has either died or will surely have forgotten me by now."

"You have been gone months, not years, Andrés, and I doubt anyone could forget you."

"I am quite content with being your cabin boy, Captain."

He pulled off his boots and dropped them next to the bed. "One day that will change."

"I can assure you, Captain, that is the one thing in my life that will never change."

Lying on top of the blankets, he rested his hands behind his head. "Never be so sure, boy."

Annie sighed. "Which book should I read?"

He shut his eyes. "Surprise me."

After she picked one, Annie hopped on the foot of his bed. Her quick bounce made the captain open one eye.

"Which one did you choose?" he asked.

"*Roxana* by Daniel Defoe. I assume it is about a girl."

He bolted upright, snatched the book from Annie's hands and hastily slipped it under his pillow.

"Captain, you told me to surprise you."

"That you did, boy," he said. "But I shall burn in Hades if I let you read that book. Besides, you wouldn't like it. The poor woman died destitute and alone as I recall."

"Oh, that will never do. I don't want to read you a sad tale." She went back to his library. "What about this one? Works by Thomas Dekker." Annie held up the book.

"Ah, one of my favorites."

Before she could hop back on his bed, Captain Hawke pointed across the room, "Andrés, sit over there."

Annie plopped down into the needlepoint armchair and began reading passages from *Old Fortunatus*, "... and a wise man poor is like a sacred book that's never read; to himself he lives and to all else seems dead..."

With his eyes shut, the captain recited the next line, "This age thinks better of a gilded fool, than of a threadbare saint in Wisdom's school."

As her nightly readings continued, Annie realized Captain Hawke had memorized numerous verses and chapters from his beloved collection. Once his interruptions ceased, he had fallen asleep, signaling Annie to tiptoe out of his cabin.

On the last night before they were to drop anchor in England, Annie sat with a half-read book on her lap. As she listened to the captain's soft snoring, she wondered who would read to him if she were not his cabin boy. Mr. Montgomery? No, she thought, Captain Hawke was too proud a man to have his first mate read to him, even though she learned it was Mr. Montgomery who had taught him to read. But since I will always be his cabin boy, I needn't worry.

CHAPTER THIRTY-FIVE

Leaning on the larboard rail, Annie waited for the sailors to put the gangway down. She turned to the first mate. "After we visit Christopher's mum, will you be visiting your family, Mr. Montgomery?"

"I will put off that happy reunion for as long as I can."

"I would think you would be anxious to see them."

"My brothers say I am an embarrassment to our family. Father wonders when I will give up this foolishness. And despite the fact that Mother loves Captain Hawke, she can be equally annoying. She is forever asking me when will I get married."

"Uh, what was that about your mother loving Captain Hawke?" Annie asked.

Mr. Montgomery laughed. "Mother can't help but love the man who saved her son's life."

"The captain saved your life?"

"In fact, he saved my life twice." Mr. Montgomery pointed across from the wharf. "The first time was over in that alley when I was ten years old. Father used to bring me here to look at the ships. But when he took ill one Sunday, I came by myself."

He chuckled. "My driver was too busy imbibing to notice me being dragged off into the alley by two hooligans."

Annie shivered at the sight of the alley, the same one where she had spent two chilly nights. She asked, "You must have fought back?"

"Hard to fight back when someone is holding a knife to your throat while the other one is pulling off your boots."

"No matter what, I can't imagine you not putting up a fight."

"You flatter me, lad, but back then I was scrawny and short. The captain had an advantage of having lived on the streets."

"If you were ten, how old was he?" Annie asked.

"About my age, but back then, he was taller than me. He came out of nowhere, whipped them both, took their weapons and told me I should do myself a favor and stay away from the docks."

"He thought my boots were small payment for saving my life. I agreed. Ten years passed before we met again. Hard to believe that was only three years ago. A lot has happened since then."

"Did you recognize him when you saw him again?" Annie wondered if Abigail would recognize her after only a few months of being separated.

"Aye, I recognized him. He was a taller, older version of the boy who had saved my life the first time."

"What about the second rescue? Did it happen at the docks, too?" Annie asked.

"No, out at sea," Mr. Montgomery said as he picked

up the satchel lying at his feet.

"You can't stop there."

"One day, you will hear the whole story, but not now."

"At least tell me this, what did the captain get for saving your life a second time, two pairs of boots?" Annie laughed.

"No, Andrés." Mr. Montgomery smiled. "He got this ship."

CHAPTER THIRTY-SIX

Once Annie and Mr. Montgomery disembarked, they made their way to Philip's Livery Stable. The first mate looked over the horses in the stalls before picking one that looked anxious for a good run.

"Wise choice, sir. 'E's a lively one, but you look like you can 'andle 'im," the stable boy said. As he led the horse out of the stall, he eyed Annie. "I will get you the grey mare."

Mr Montgomery patted his horse's neck. "You do know how to ride, don't you, Andrés?" he asked.

Standing on a mounting block, Annie placed her hand on the pommel and hoisted herself onto the saddle. "Of course, I do, sir."

Annie chuckled to herself, thinking how Mr. Montgomery would be flabbergasted if he knew she had only ridden sidesaddle.

* * *

Annie trotted behind Mr. Montgomery on the meandering ride through the countryside. With images of Christopher playing over and over in her head, Annie observed little of the rise and fall of the landscape.

Mr. Montgomery waved Annie to come up alongside him. "This is not the first time I will be bringing bad news to a sailor's wife or mother, and it won't be my last," he said to her. "Remember, you must keep your own emotions under control. I will do most of the talking. When you talk to Christopher's mother, make sure you are ready. We don't want to make this anymore difficult than it already is. Do you understand?"

"I think so," Annie said.

Together, they neared a cottage where wildflowers wove their way through a small vegetable garden.

A dog greeted them with no more than a lift of his head and a sweep of his tail sending puffs of dust into the air.

After dismounting, Annie knelt down to pet the dog. "Good boy, Jasper. Christopher said you..."

"You know my son?" The voice came from the cottage doorway.

Like Jasper, Christopher's mother was plump and gray. After brief introductions, she warmly invited them in. Annie hesitated in the doorway, her hands clammy.

The cottage was much like the one she had lived in with her uncle's family, only smaller and in desperate need of repair. The blackened ceiling sagged, but the furniture was solid and welcoming.

Even though there was no chill in the air, Mrs. Doyle pulled her shawl tightly around her shoulders. "You say you are shipmates of my son, but where is he?"

"I believe you should sit down, Mrs. Doyle," Mr.

Montgomery said in a firm yet compassionate voice. "I am sorry, but we bring bad news about your son,"

Seeing the woman sway, Annie grabbed her elbow. With Annie and Mr. Montgomery's support, Mrs. Doyle staggered to a chair.

"Has Christopher taken ill? That boy was always getting sick, you know."

"I am afraid he did take ill shortly after we left the colonies." Mr. Montgomery said.

While Mr. Montgomery's story unfolded, Annie realized Mrs. Doyle wouldn't be learning the true nature of her son's death. Mr. Montgomery's tale ended with, "I assure you that Christopher died peacefully in his sleep."

Whether he died a gruesome death or in his sleep, Christopher was dead. Nothing would change that fact, and Annie knew his mother would grieve for him for the rest of her life.

Tears ran down Mrs. Doyle's cheeks as she motioned to a wooden bench. "Sit, please. Christopher would want his friends to stay for biscuits." With trembling hands, she stroked the oak table. "He made this all by himself."

While Annie fought back tears, Mr. Montgomery remained stoic. He ran his hand along the smooth grain of the wood. "We all admired Christopher's wood carvings on the ship, but I had no idea he was such a skilled craftsman. You must have been very proud of him."

"I have always been proud of Christopher. I

thought he would be a cabinetmaker like his father, but he had other plans," Mrs. Doyle said. "I never thought anyone would hire him as a sailor, him being a cripple and all. He was born that way, you know, one leg shorter than the other and that one foot of his never quite caught up with the other. Nothin' we could do about it, and he never let it get in the way of what he wanted to do. When he told me Captain Hawke hired him, I can't ever remember seeing Christopher that happy.

"I missed him terribly, but I never thought it would be…" She looked up, her mouth agape. "Forever."

Mr. Montgomery patted Mrs. Doyle's hand before reaching into his satchel. He handed her Christopher's Bible and then a letter. "This is from Captain Hawke. He thought a great deal of your son."

Mrs. Doyle took the letter and began reading it to herself. When she struggled with a word, which was often, she asked Mr. Montgomery for help.

Annie listened to the muffled sobs coming from Christopher's mother as she read the letter to herself. Annie's heart was breaking, too, as she waited for the right moment to tell Mrs. Doyle how much Christopher had loved her. The woman continued reading and then stopped. She looked up, puzzled.

"Such kind words from your captain, but I don't understand…"

"What is it that you don't understand, Mrs. Doyle?" Mr. Montgomery said gently.

"He speaks of a girl who was with my Christopher

when he died. How is that possible?"

"A girl? There are no girls on the Realm." Mr. Montgomery appeared equally confused. "Only Andrés and our surgeon were with Christopher the day he died. I am sure there is a logical explanation. If you don't mind, may I see the letter?"

"Certainly," she said as she pointed to a passage. "Captain Hawke said her hair was black as a moonless night and her eyes the palest blue, but he never mentions her name."

Mr. Montgomery looked at Annie. "Do you have any idea who the captain is talking about?"

Annie shook her head while she gnawed on her lower lip. She felt her knees go weak when she heard Mr. Montgomery read aloud.

"Christopher shared an innocent kiss with the lovely maiden. She stayed by his side until he drew his last breath.

"I am sorry, Mrs. Doyle," Mr. Montgomery said. "But apparently Captain Hawke is privy to matters I know nothing about."

Although Mr. Montgomery appeared visibly shaken by the turn of events, he still managed to stay on task. He took money from his satchel and laid it on the table. "I am sure you know that Christopher saved most of his wages for you. However, some of this is from the proceeds collected at an auction that was held in your son's honor.

"And Captain Hawke wants you to know that any debts you might have will be taken care of."

Overwhelmed, Mrs. Doyle hugged Mr.

Montgomery. She then turned to Annie and squeezed her hand. "You have been rather quiet, dear. Did you know my son well?"

"Yes, ma'am. He was a mighty fine sailor and a dear friend. Christopher wanted you to know how much he loved you, but you already knew that."

Mrs. Doyle pulled Annie closer to her. Annie tugged on her shirt button while Christopher's mother stared deep into her ice-blue eyes. Mrs. Doyle pushed the rim of Annie's cap just high enough to reveal the slight curve of her eyebrows. With her head tilted to the side, Mrs. Doyle ran a thumb along the inside of Annie's cap.

"It is much too hot in here for you to be wearing this."

Before Annie could object, Mrs. Doyle pulled the cap off her head. Annie's dark hair fell across one eye. She wanted to run, but found it impossible to move.

Mrs. Doyle's voice cracked. "Mr. Montgomery said you were with Christopher when he died. Your hair and eyes are just like the girl's that the captain described in his letter. Tell me your name, your real name."

"My name is...Annie."

Mrs. Doyle put her hand to her lips. "Did...did you love my son?"

Annie answered truthfully. "Yes, I loved Christopher. Everyone loved your son."

Mrs. Doyle stood back and studied Annie. "How long did Christopher know you were a girl?"

"I would like to hear the answer to that question myself." Mr. Montgomery's voice shook.

"That night, he only knew that night." Annie looked from Mr. Montgomery to Mrs. Doyle.

While Mr. Montgomery looked pale and shocked, Mrs. Doyle appeared content.

"Please, I want to know everything about your friendship with my son and his days on the Realm," she said.

Annie sat down beside her. She described Christopher's life at sea and spared no details. While they shared tears and laughter about the friend and son they both loved, Annie glanced at Mr. Montgomery who sat in stony silence.

Seeming frailer than when Annie and Mr. Montgomery first arrived, Mrs. Doyle got up from the table. "Thank you, Annie, for being a part of Christopher's life. I wish to be alone now."

Mrs. Doyle managed a tiny smile. "Mr. Montgomery, thank you for your visit and please tell your captain I appreciate everything he had done for my Christopher."

* * *

Annie untied her horse from the privet bush. Not wishing to ask Mr. Montgomery for assistance, she attempted to pull herself into the saddle. She dangled for a second before giving up. Dust circled her feet where she landed.

She then decided that charging from several paces away would be her only hope of scaling the mare.

Annie dashed toward the old horse. She leaped for the saddle, but fell short, succeeding only in spooking the animal.

Watching her unsuccessful attempt, Mr. Montgomery quickly grabbed the reins as the horse reared up. "Whoa!"

Once he calmed the horse down, he called to Annie. "Get over here, Andrés, Annie, or whatever your name might be."

"I prefer Andrés, sir."

Mr. Montgomery used his hands as a mounting block for her. She placed one foot in his palms as he lifted Annie high enough to pull herself onto the saddle.

Mr. Montgomery stared at Annie, no words spoken. He shook his head before mounting his horse and galloped off.

Annie was left in a swirling cloud of dust and confusion. Unable to catch up, Annie could only hope he would be waiting for her at the stable.

* * *

Returning to the livery stable, Annie found Mr. Montgomery leaning against a stall. Her relief was short-lived.

He smacked a riding crop against his leg before tossing it in the hay. "I fulfilled the captain's orders. We took care of Christopher's mother and you are back safely."

Mr. Montgomery turned his back to Annie and marched out of the stable.

After dropping from the saddle, Annie handed the reins to the stable boy. She ran off to join Mr. Montgomery.

"Why are you so angry?" she called after him.

He reeled around. "Are you serious? I am such a fool. I dispelled rumors about you being a girl. Yet, Captain Hawke, Doc, and Christopher all knew you were a girl. I am beginning to think I am the only one on the Realm who didn't know the truth."

"If it helps, Mr. Montgomery, those are the only people who knew."

"How long has Captain Hawke and Doc known?"

"Doc learned the first day I came aboard. Captain Hawke? I don't know for certain. It might have been the night Christopher died. Whenever it was, he never let on that he knew."

Mr. Montgomery raised his eyebrows at her. "Did you really kiss Christopher?"

Annie blushed. "Aye, not a romantic kiss, but I think it made him happy."

"I am sure it did. So, what do I call you Andrés or Annie?"

Annie kicked a rock in her path. "Andrés. I am a Jack-tar. Nothing will change that." She headed back to the Realm.

"Wait." Mr. Montgomery said. "Come with me... Andrés. We need to talk."

CHAPTER THIRTY-SEVEN

They hadn't walked far when Mr. Montgomery pulled Annie out of the way of the foot traffic. "I have so many questions. I don't know where to begin."

"Like you told me that first night in port," Annie said. "Everyone on the Realm is running away from someone or something. I am no exception."

"True, but I can assure you, this is a first," he said as he pointed his opened hands at her.

Without further prompting, Annie said, "My aunt blamed me for my uncle's death. She said I was cursed. I had no other choice but to run away."

Mr. Montgomery slipped his finger under Annie's chin, slightly tilting her head back. "She did more than simply calling you cursed. Am I right?"

Annie pushed his hand away. "She whipped me, Mr. Montgomery, and it wasn't the first time. I feared for my life."

"I gather you had no other family or friends to turn to."

"No one," Annie said.

"But why on earth would you pretend to be a boy."

"It was both my cousin's and my idea. He said it was too dangerous for a girl to be alone in London, that I should dress up like a boy. And I always loved

201

the sea—so what better way to hide than on a ship. The Realm has become my home, Mr. Montgomery."

"But I am not certain it can remain your home. Now that I know, I won't be able to think of you as Andrés ever again."

"If Doc and, apparently, the captain could keep it a secret, surely you can, Mr. Montgomery."

He shook his head from side to side and sighed. "I just don't know…Andrés. I just don't know."

Suddenly, a smile replaced the frown on his face. "My, my," he said, "It has been a long time since I have seen anything quite so exquisite."

Annie's shoulders relaxed at the sound of Mr. Montgomery's buoyant voice. She tried to see what had distracted him. "What are you looking at, sir?"

He pointed across the street.

Annie craned her neck. "I still don't know what you are looking at."

"How can you not see her?" Mr. Montgomery said.

"Oh, so it is a woman I should be looking for."

Annie looked between the horse-drawn drays and wagons traveling on the cobblestone street. She eventually saw, not one, but three young women. "Hmm, ladies of their social standing should not be here amongst beggars, drunkards and the worst rabble of all—sailors," Annie said.

Mr. Montgomery laughed. "Perhaps I should do something about that."

"Perhaps, you should."

Annie continued observing the young women.

"The two shorter women look like they expect to be robbed at any moment, which is a distinct possibility. We all know London is full of thieves. But I wager it is the tall one who has caught your fancy, Mr. Montgomery. Am I correct?"

"Aye, she is the one. Wish she would turn around so I could see her face."

Wisps of strawberry blond hair caught the sunlight. Wearing a yellow dress, she towered over her friends.

"Do you wish to meet her, sir?"

"I certainly do." Mr. Montgomery straightened his jacket. "She is a beauty."

"And how can you possibly know that, sir? We can't even see her face."

"Look how she carries herself. No woman that tall would stand with such confidence unless she was beautiful."

"You have always been a keen observer, Mr. Montgomery."

He took a step back, stared at Annie while stroking his clean-shaven chin. "Hmm."

Annie fidgeted with her button. "Mr. Montgomery, is something wrong?"

"Straighten your collar. Tuck in that shirt." He grinned. "You know, you are rather nice looking, in a street urchin sort of way."

"What are you thinking, Mr. Montgomery?"

"What I'm thinking is that I bet those young women cannot resist a charming little fellow like you. I know the captain couldn't. Now pull your cap back a bit and let some of your hair fall into your face."

Mr. Montgomery took a handkerchief from his pocket and spit on it. "Always worked for my mother. Stand still," he said while he rubbed some of the dirt from Annie's face. "That will have to do. Now go over there, be your charming self and tell that lovely lady I wish to meet her. Perhaps something can be salvaged from this dreadful day."

Annie thought Mr. Montgomery was quite out of his mind, but followed his orders nonetheless. She wound her way between the conveyances and approached the young women.

Doffing her cap, Annie announced, "Ladies, that handsome gentleman across the street wishes to make your acquaintance." She emphasized the word handsome while pointing toward Mr. Montgomery.

The taller of the three didn't even glance at Annie while she strained her neck to see the man Annie spoke of. Mr. Montgomery tipped his tricorn hat at her when he caught her eye.

The statuesque beauty glanced at Annie, but only for an instant. Annie gulped hard when she saw a hint of a smile form on the young woman's lips as she looked back at Mr. Montgomery.

"I gather you mean the gentleman with the silly grin on his face. Why should we make his acquaintance?" She inquired.

Impossible to stay focused on Mr. Montgomery, Annie stared up into Abigail Spencer's face, the young woman Annie had been maid and companion to for eight years. Annie stammered. "B-because he—he is a fine gentleman and you are, in his words: exquisite."

The lady continued gazing at the first mate. "Does he not think my friends are exquisite as well?"

Annie looked at the two shorter women. She recognized them, too, Hannah and Catherine Cudney. She remembered how the sisters' annoying laughter bounced off the walls during their infrequent visits to Spencer Manor.

While the Cudney sisters gawked at Mr. Montgomery, they showed little interest in the ragamuffin delivering the message. Annie hoped no one noticed the red creeping up her neck.

She addressed Abigail, "He he believes your friends are both lovely, milady. But 'tis you, he is quite t-taken with."

Their eyes met. Abigail studied Annie's dirt-smudged face, chafed hands and broken fingernails. She brushed Annie's hair away from her flushed cheek. This time it was her turn to stutter. "Wh-what is your name?"

CHAPTER THIRTY-EIGHT

Abigail didn't have to say another word for Annie to know that her two worlds had collided. She pulled her cap on so low her eyelashes skimmed the edge when she blinked. She wished she could have pulled the cap down to her knees.

Annie drew in a deep breath and stared down at her boots. "M-my name is Andrés de la Cruz, m-milady."

"HImm, why does that name sound familiar? Oh, now I remember. A girl, who once worked for me, talked about a grandfather by that name. Well, *Andrés de la Cruz*, tell me more about the gentleman."

"The gentleman?"

"Yes, you heard me. Tell me more about the gentleman."

Abigail leaned down, saying loud enough for only Annie to hear, "I see you wish to play dress-up. And while I do not understand why you are doing this, I will play along with you for the moment. The gentleman, tell me about him."

"Uh, Mr. Montgomery is a delightful bloke, a little too chatty at times, but he is well-bred," Annie said.

"Like one of my father's hounds?"

"No, more like one of your brothers. I mean if you

had brothers. Mr. Montgomery is an Oxford gentleman and like I said before, he is quite handsome."

She glanced across the street at Mr. Montgomery. "I must admit, your gentleman friend is not bad on the eyes. Fetch him for me."

Annie hurried back across the street. She caught her breath. "Mr. Montgomery, she wants to meet you."

* * *

"Ladies, let me introduce myself. I am Mr. Matthew Montgomery, first mate of the merchant ship, the Realm."

Abigail glared at him. "Should I be impressed?"

Annie expected his smile to disappear. Instead, it looked pasted on his face. To help him out, she quickly added, "Mr. Montgomery is second in command on the Realm. If anything should happen to our captain, he would be in charge."

The Cudney sisters gushed. "Oh, my."

"I am pleased to make your acquaintance, Mr. Montgomery," Abigail finally said. "I am Abigail Spencer, daughter of Lord and Lady Spencer of Surrey County. Perhaps, you have met my father. He ships some of his goods to the American colonies."

"I don't believe I have had the pleasure," he said. "Perhaps, you have met my father, Roger Montgomery, Earl of Leeds."

Annie detected the subtle widening of Abigail's eyes and parting of her full lips.

"May I offer you and your friends some advice?" Mr. Montgomery said. "If you wish to be in this part of

London, you should be escorted."

Abigail gestured to a man standing in a doorway not far from where they stood. He looked quite dapper in his green braided coat, breeches and white silk stockings. "We are indeed escorted, Mr. Montgomery. That is my footman, Robert. Do not let his casual manner deceive you. It would be unwise to make any improper advances toward me," she warned.

"Abigail," Hannah said. "The gentleman is right. Escorted or not, we should never be at this dreadful place,"

"Dreadful," Catherine agreed. "Someone emptied a chamber pot from their second floor window. It just missed us."

Hannah dusted off her dress. "And the soot from the factories and tenements disgusting."

"Disgusting," Catherine concurred.

"Why do you ladies come here if it displeases you so?" Mr. Montgomery asked.

Catherine wrinkled her nose. "Abigail's maid ran off months ago and she has made us come down here five, maybe six times to look for her. The girl's cousin told Abigail she had gone to London. He specifically said the docks, something about the girl having fond memories of the sea." She stuck her nose up in the air. "You just can't find good help these days."

Hannah laughed. "But I must admit 'tis great fun fooling our parents. They think we are spending another day at Spencer Manor while Lord and Lady Spencer believe Abigail is with us at our estate."

"All this because a *maid* ran away," Mr. Montgomery said.

Looking him straight in the eye, Abigail stood toe to toe with the first mate. "Don't look so skeptical, Mr. Montgomery. She was never simply my maid. She was my companion, my best friend."

"Do you know why she left?" he asked.

Abigail scowled down at Annie. "Would you care to venture a guess?"

Annie avoided her gaze. "I am but a lowly Jack-tar, milady. It would not be my place to say."

Abigail rolled her eyes. "Oh, please!"

"Well, at least the lad knows *his* place," Hannah said.

Her sister nodded in agreement. "Abigail's maid never knew her place."

Annie believed it was time Abigail heard the truth. "Perhaps your maid did know her place. Perhaps, that is why she never asked you for your help. Perhaps..."

Abigail took Annie's hand. "Perhaps, she was wrong."

For an instant, Annie was a child again, running and laughing in the Spencer's rose garden with her best friend. She slowly pulled away.

Mr. Montgomery looked from Abigail to Annie and back to Abigail again. "Why do I get the feeling you two know each other?"

With her eyes trained on Annie, Abigail answered, "Why don't you ask *Andrés*? Or should I say, Annie?"

"Did you say 'Annie'?" Mr. Montgomery asked.

"Yes, she did. I am the maid that Abigail spoke of," Annie replied.

The Cudney sisters gasped. Together, they took a step back as if Annie were carrying the plague.

"Abigail?" Mr. Montgomery said. "I knew that name sounded familiar. She spoke of you in Charles Town."

Abigail clutched her hands to her heart and looked at Annie. "You did? What did you say about me?"

Annie looked down at her boots and murmured, "I can't recall what I said."

"Mr. Montgomery, can you remember what she said about me? I will cherish those words forever."

"She said you were tall," he said.

Abigail put her hands on her hips. "Tall? That's it?"

Annie looked up. "I can explain."

"Don't bother," Abigail said. She turned to Mr. Montgomery. "I am surprised you do not appear all that shocked that Andrés is really Annie."

"Yesterday, I knew Annie only as Andrés. Today, it has been one surprise after another. I think I am still in shock. I doubt any new revelation about Captain Hawke's cabin boy will surprise me ever again."

Hannah and Catherine's mouths dropped open. "Cabin boy?" they said.

Annie had enough. "I need to return to the ship," she said. "I think my head is about to explode."

"You *need* to come back with me to Spencer Manor," Abigail said.

"If you were truly my friend, you never would ask

me to return to Aunt Mary."

"Annie, I am not asking you to return to your aunt. Please, let me explain." Abigail reached out to her.

Keeping her from grabbing Annie, Mr. Montgomery seized Abigail's arm.

As Annie hurried off, she turned in time to see Abigail's footman leap into action. Mr. Montgomery can take care of himself, she thought, as she continued her way back to the ship.

CHAPTER THIRTY-NINE

After rushing up the gangway, Annie sprinted across the deck to the hatch and bounded down the ladder. Breathless, she burst into Captain Hawke's cabin.

"How long have you known?"

He pushed back from the gate-leg table. "Did you forget to knock?"

Sitting across from the captain was Doc. Annie locked eyes with him. He continued pouring a cup of tea until his cup overflowed. He jerked his hand away.

"You told him!"

Doc wiped the hot liquid from his hand. "What on earth are you talking about?"

Annie gestured toward Captain Hawke. "He knows everything, that I'm a girl, that I kissed Christopher. You must have told him."

Captain Hawke didn't wait for Doc to reply. "He told me you were a girl shortly after we left for the colonies."

Annie screamed at Doc. "You promised me you would never tell him!"

"I promised you no such thing," Doc said. "I believe my words were something like, 'I have a plan.'"

"I was not aware your plan involved telling the

captain."

Captain Hawke broke in again. "Doc kept your secret for as long as he could. When I told him you had to move into the men's quarters, he had no choice but to tell me the truth."

Annie thought a moment. "You were so angry the morning you found me in the fo'c'sle with Barrette. He thought it had nothing to do with me not bringing you your breakfast and being late to report to Mr. Allan. He was right, wasn't he? It all makes sense now—the hammock, everything. I'm right, aren't I?"

"Aye. Doc told me during our chess game the night before I found you in the fo'c'sle. But how did you find out I knew?"

Annie's fury diminished when she thought about the words in the letter to Mrs. Doyle. "Christopher's mother figured out you were describing me in the letter."

He frowned. "I wanted to rewrite that letter, but with my eyesight going bad…"

Mr. Montgomery stood in the doorway. He waved his hands in the air before slamming the door shut behind him.

"Has everyone forgotten it is proper to knock?" Captain Hawke said.

"Is it *proper* that you neglected to tell me that Andrés is a girl and that your eyesight has gone bad? What else have you kept from me?"

"I think that about sums it up." The captain tapped the side of his face. "Have you been in a fight?"

Mr. Montgomery reached up to where a bruise was forming on his cheek. "Not a fight, a misunderstanding with Abigail's footman. I didn't see it coming, but we're good now."

"Who's Abigail?"

Mr. Montgomery raised his voice. "Never mind about Abigail. I want to know when were you going to tell me that Andrés was a girl, Jonathan?"

"Never," the captain said.

"Never?"

"I felt it would be safer for her if none of the crew knew."

"I am not simply a member of your crew, Jonathan. Have you forgotten who gave you this bloody ship?"

"You gave me this ship, because I saved your bloody life."

While the two traded barbs, Annie wondered what other things she would learn.

Mr. Montgomery struck the table with his fist. "Knowing she was a girl, how could you have allowed her to board the Margaret Louise? She could have been killed."

"It was poor judgement on your part to let a cabin boy, any cabin boy, be in your boarding party," Captain Hawke said.

"I paired her with me for that reason, Jonathan," Mr. Montgomery said.

Annie looked at Captain Hawke. "So that's why you asked me those questions after I came down from the mast. You were trying to delay me. You were worried I might get on that boarding party."

Before Captain Hawke could comment, Mr. Montgomery said to Annie, "I never would have let you take Barrette's place if the captain had trusted me."

"I did what I thought was best," Captain Hawke said.

Annie needed time to collect her thoughts. She slipped out of the cabin and headed for the fo'c'sle.

CHAPTER FORTY

Adding to Annie's frustration, the fo'c'sle wasn't empty. One sailor remained, Barrette. Annie watched while he searched through his sea chest. Whatever he was looking for, she hoped he would hurry up and find it.

He pulled out a white linen shirt. Barrette tossed it to Annie while he unbuttoned the one he wore. She caught the shirt before it floated to the deck.

"You think the ladies will like it, Andrés?"

"Aye."

"Are you all right, mate? You don't look well."

"I-I'm fine. It's just, just that I visited Christopher's mum today," she said as she tried hard not to stare at Barrette's bare chest.

"Poor woman. How did she take it?"

"Better than I thought she would."

"Good. My shirt, Andrés, hand it back." Barrette snapped his fingers. "Did you hear me, Andrés? Hand me the shirt."

While Annie stared at Barrette's muscles and hairless chest, goose bumps rose on her arms. "Did you say something?" she asked.

He grabbed the shirt from Annie and stuck his arm through its billowy sleeve. "Do you want to come along

217

with me? I am meeting Baggott and Carter in town."

Annie stretched. "It has been a most exhausting day. I would rather stay here."

"I don't believe you."

"What is there not to believe?"

"You will not go into town with me, because I am not Mr. Montgomery. I'm right. Aren't I?"

"What are you talking about?"

Barrette folded his arms across his chest. "You only leave this ship with our esteemed first mate and I wager it is Captain Hawke who orders it. Why is that, Andrés? What makes *you* so special?"

"You are insane, Barrette."

"You are not fooling me." He headed for the passageway. "If you change your mind, I will be at the Black Anchor Pub."

Annie thought to herself, I'm not fooling myself, either. I know what I want.

* * *

Annie went back to Captain Hawke's cabin. She didn't hesitate as she pounded on the door.

"Come in."

Across the cabin, Captain Hawke pulled up a chair and began shuffling through papers on his desk. He looked up at Annie. "So kind of you to knock this time. As you can see, I am terribly busy"

Annie slapped her hand in the middle of the papers. "Don't pretend you are reading these papers, Captain. I know better."

He gestured to a chair. "Take a seat, please."

Annie couldn't remember Captain Hawke ever addressing her with such niceties before, but all that mattered now was that he remembered who she was. "There is no other way to put this, Captain. I want to remain your cabin boy."

"Are you certain this is what Annie wants?" The captain reached over, and plucked the cap from her head.

She snatched it back, pulling it defiantly over her ears. "I don't even know who Annie is anymore."

"Then maybe you should find out who she is before making any hasty decisions," the captain said. "But once I tell the crew that you are a girl, it will not make much difference who you think you are."

"Please, Captain, I beg of you, don't tell them."

"Andrés no longer exists. He never did, Annie. You never belonged here."

"I do belong here!" Annie tugged on her shirt button until the threads snapped. "I can tie every kind of knot from a catspaw to a timber-hitch. I have tended the livestock, worked in the galley and shortened sails. Look..." She pointed to the palm of her right hand. "That is a burn from tarring ropes. You said I needed to earn the respect of the crew, and I have done just that. I deserve to be here."

He drummed his fingers on the mahogany desk. "I will hold off telling the crew for now."

"Thank you, Captain." One small victory, Annie thought.

"Tomorrow morning at nine, you and Mr.

Montgomery will meet Abigail Spencer at St. Paul's Cathedral under the clock tower."

Annie's button tumbled from her fingertips, rolling across the floor striking the captain's boot. "Why?" she asked.

"Mr. Montgomery made the arrangements with Miss Spencer before he returned to the Realm. And don't even think of not going. I am ordering you to go."

"I beg your pardon, Captain, but there is no reason why I should meet Abigail tomorrow or any day."

"You are still in Lord Spencer's employ."

Annie protested. "There is no contract."

"You earned money as maid and companion to his daughter. How many years was that...eight?"

She glared at him. "Why ask when you already know the answer?"

"Then it is settled," he said

"Does this mean I am no longer your cabin boy?"

Captain Hawke picked up the button lying by his boot and pressed it into Annie's hand. "What it means is this: If you ever return to this ship, you better know who you are."

With a flick of his wrist, he dismissed her.

* * *

Needing to be alone, Annie returned to the abandoned fo'c'sle where she sat for hours before going to Doc's quarters. She slowly pushed open the door. The familiar creak didn't wake him. Doc wasn't asleep.

"The captain wants me to leave."

"Annie, he doesn't want you to leave any more than

I do, but he does want what is best for you."

"It is not up to him to decide what is best for me. I can't leave the Realm. I can't leave you, Doc. You have been like a father to me. This is where I belong."

"If I were your father, I would tell you that Abigail and you have some lost time to make up. Mr. Montgomery told me that Abigail thought of you more than simply her maid. Now get some sleep, Annie."

Like her first night on the Realm, the ship was nearly deserted, but Annie had no need to explore the decks. She knew every nook and cranny, every smell, every movement and sound of the ship. She lie awake, afraid to close her eyes, afraid of what the morning would bring

CHAPTER FORTY-ONE

After a restless night, Annie dozed off in the carriage.

Mr. Montgomery lightly shook her shoulder. "Annie, wake up. We will walk the rest of the way."

Yawning as she stepped out of the carriage, Annie dragged her feet behind Mr. Montgomery. He kept glancing back at her as if he expected her to bolt at any moment. But the closer they came to the clock tower, Annie realized she was eager to see Abigail again.

Mr. Montgomery's outstretched arm, brought her to an abrupt halt.

"Why are we stopping?" she asked.

"Look at her, Annie. Isn't she a vision of loveliness?" Mr. Montgomery said while watching Abigail pace back and forth under the clock tower.

He let out a long sigh when Abigail paused to primp the strawberry blond curls around her face. "She is waiting for you, Annie," Mr. Montgomery said.

"I am certain she wants to see you as badly as she wants to see me, sir."

"I will join you shortly. Now go!"

"Aye, aye, sir!"

Racing to Abigail, Annie repeated, "Beg your pardon," to the people she bumped into on the crowded walk. With her arms outstretched to embrace Abigail, Annie didn't see the man coming up behind her.

Annie's legs went out from under her when he seized her, lifting Annie off the ground.

Mr. Montgomery was there in a flash. He wrapped his arm across the assailant's shoulders. "Unhand her!"

"Her?" the man said as he let Annie go.

Mr. Montgomery slammed the man to the ground, placing his boot squarely on the man's chest, the tip of his sword at his throat.

"Not you again!" Robert, Abigail's footman said.

"Sorry, mate, I didn't realize it was you. But then again, I would say we are now even," Mr. Montgomery said as he slid his sword back into its leather sheath. He offered his hand to Robert. "Let me help you up."

"If you don't mind, I will get up by myself."

Mr. Montgomery backed off.

"You remember Annie, don't you Robert?" Abigail asked.

"Annie, Annie Moore? Well, I'll be! It is you. I saw you yesterday, but I didn't recognize you then, either, the way you were dressed and all. And it's not my place to ask Miss Spencer her business." He scratched his head as he eyed Annie's clothes. "Why are dressed like that?"

With more than a hint of bitterness in her voice, Abigail answered for Annie, "She has been working as a sailor these last few months."

"What is this world coming to? They hire female

sailors now?"

"I can assure you, we don't. It is a long story," Mr. Montgomery said while he watched Robert pat down his jacket and breeches. "I hope I didn't harm you,"

"I am quite alright."

"Annie and Mr. Montgomery will be my guests at Spencer Manor today, Robert," Abigail said.

She turned to Annie. "Let me look at you. You look simply…I am at a loss for words."

"You are never at a loss for words, Abigail," Annie said.

Abigail sniffed the air. "Couldn't you have at least bathed? Why is it that Mr. Montgomery smells of sweet violets? And his clothes are immaculate. Is that silk?"

Mr. Montgomery stroked his tan waistcoat and murmured, "Yes, it is."

"Unlike me, Abigail, Mr. Montgomery is quite civilized. I would wager he doused himself with cologne just for you," Annie said.

"Is that true, Mr. Montgomery?" Abigail purred. "Oh my, are you blushing? I would not think the son of an earl could be so easily embarrassed."

"I thought you did not believe me when I told you about my father," Mr. Montgomery said.

"Oh, I didn't," Abigail replied. "But I asked my father some questions about the Earl of Leeds. Apparently, he has three sons. Like my brothers, they are all Oxford scholars, even his wayward son. I assume that the wayward son is you, Mr. Montgomery?"

He bowed chivalrously. "Wayward son at your service, milady."

Abigail turned her attention back to Annie. "I bet you have some exciting stories to tell me."

Annie rubbed her arm. "Which one would you like me to tell you first? When I got shot or when my friend was impaled by a yardarm."

"I have no idea what a yardarm is. Nor do I want to know." Abigail sighed. "Why would you make up such ghastly tales, to shock me? No matter, you are back and everything will be as it once was."

"I am not making up tales. I told you before, I will never go back to Aunt Mary," Annie said.

"Before you ran off yesterday, I tried to tell you that Erik told Father how your aunt had mistreated you all those years. When Father found out what she had done, he dismissed her."

"I never would have thought Erik would turn against his mother."

"It was not easy for him, but when Father asked him what had become of you, he could not lie." Abigail smiled warmly. "Not Erik."

"No, not Erik." Annie agreed.

"Father paid your aunt a tidy sum for her and her younger sons to leave Surrey County and never come back. Father, however, told Erik he could continue working for our groom, Anthony. Your aunt threatened to have the constable on my father for making Erik stay at our estate, but Father knew it was an empty threat. She looked too happy when he handed her the money.

So, you can return without fear of being harmed. Isn't that wonderful?"

"I suppose so," Annie said, but quickly added. "But only for a visit."

CHAPTER FORTY-TWO

Before departing to Spencer Manor, Mr. Montgomery brought up an issue that needed immediate attention. He eyed Annie out of the corner of his eye, while he held out a leather drawstring purse to Abigail. "Captain Hawke hoped you would be so kind as to help Annie pick out a dress."

Annie waved her arms in the air as if she were battling a swarm of bees. "A dress. Never!"

"Oh, Annie, this shall be great fun." Abigail said.

"For you, maybe, but not me. Dresses are quite impractical."

Abigail laughed. "You are so silly."

"The captain wants Annie to have only the best." Mr. Montgomery's gaze shifted to Annie's boots. "And shoes, a fine lady must have appropriate footwear."

"The captain is a fine one to talk about fashion. He dresses like a drunken toad. Besides, I am not a lady," Annie said.

Her complaints went unheeded.

"Captain Hawke mentioned a dress shop on Paternoster Row," Mr. Montgomery said.

Robert assisted them into the carriage before giving the coachman their destination.

Abigail sat next to Annie. As Abigail shook the

purse, they both listened to the jingling coins. Opening it, Abigail peered inside. "Apparently, your captain has no idea how much a dress costs."

Annie tried to sound disappointed. "It is too bad there is not enough money to buy me a dress," she said.

"Oh, there are enough gold coins to buy you a dress. In fact, you can buy yourself an entire dress shop. We are going shopping." Abigail said.

The carriage rumbled along the bumpy cobblestone streets past St. Paul's Cathedral to Paternoster Row.

"There it is," Mr. Montgomery said.

A wooden sign, Marlowe's Dress Shop, swung from an iron bar. The freshly painted storefront stood out among the other shops.

"How on earth would the captain even know of this place?" Annie asked.

"No doubt he escorted one of his lady friends here," Mr. Montgomery said. "I will wait outside while you two enjoy yourselves. Now Annie, if you need me…"

"Don't worry. I doubt there are any pirates in there."

Annie looked at the love-struck first mate and turned to Abigail. "Why don't you entertain Mr. Montgomery while I go inside by myself?"

Abigail pouted. "But I wish to come with you."

She whispered to Abigail. "After you have kept Mr. Montgomery company for a few minutes, then you can join me."

"But only if you promise to at least look like you are having a good time. You look like you are going to the gallows," Abigail replied.

"I will try."

Annie stood outside the shop getting up the courage to enter. Through the window, she saw two girls in matching blue-gray dresses. One tidied up the shop while the other hunched over a ledger. A woman, her flaxen hair pulled back in a neatly pinned bun, showed an older woman some fabric.

When the transaction was finished, the woman with the golden hair walked her customer out. While the bell jingled above the door, the older woman barreled through. Annie avoided her ample figure as well as her disapproving look.

Annie didn't want to disappoint Abigail, so she sucked in her breath and entered the shop.

CHAPTER FORTY-THREE

"Good morning. How may I help you?" The shopkeeper's voice was warm and friendly.

Her greeting surprised Annie. She expected the woman to chase her out of the shop with a broom or, at the very least, fall over laughing. "I want to buy a dress," Annie said.

"You have certainly come to the right place. We have garden silks and brocades. Some of our fabrics are only twelve shillings a yard. But money is not a problem, now is it?"

"No, it isn't," Annie said.

"What do you have in mind?"

"To be honest, I haven't given it much thought. Something pretty, I suppose," Annie said. She glanced over her shoulder at the girls snickering behind her.

"Excuse me." The shopkeeper walked over to the girls and softly reprimanded them.

Returning to Annie, she asked, "Is this for a special occasion? I neglected to ask Captain Hawke when he came in earlier today." She winked at Annie. "A charmer, that one is. He was in a hurry, had some fancy lady waiting for him in an open carriage."

"Captain Hawke was here?" Annie said.

The shop girls sighed in unison every time Captain

Hawke's name was mentioned.

"I thought you knew," the shopkeeper said.

Annie shook her head.

"He did not want me to send you away when you came here, said you were to be treated like a lady. I do not mean to be rude, Miss, but it is not every day I have customers dressed like you coming into my shop." She again asked, "Is this for a special occasion?"

Annie wondered if looking like a girl again would merit a special occasion. She decided it didn't. "No," she said biting her lower lip.

"I will have you look at some bolts of fabric and then I will take your measurements," the shopkeeper said.

"I am sorry to put you through so much trouble, ma'am, but I'm afraid this is all a mistake. I don't need a dress."Annie turned to leave, but Abigail had waltzed in blocking her exit.

"Now Annie, let this nice lady do her job. The sooner you cooperate, the sooner we can leave."

Annie groaned as she reached under her shirt, wiggled a bit and then unraveled the cloth flattening her breasts. With the rag in her hand, she looked around the shop wondering where to put it.

"Do you wish to keep...that?" the shopkeeper asked.

Annie blankly stared back at her.

The shopkeeper called to one of the girls, "Christine." She pointed to the cloth. "Dispose of that, please."

The girl put down the feather duster and scrunched up her nose. With her arm outstretched, she carried the wadded material to the gutter outside. Abigail lifted her finger in the air. "I wish to have a moment with my friend."

"Certainly." The shopkeeper walked discretely to a shelf of fabric where she began straightening the rolls of material.

Abigail looked dreamily into space. "I could not wait to tell you. Mr. Montgomery is the most extraordinary man I have ever met. I could get lost in those beautiful green eyes of his. He is not simply handsome, but he is witty and intelligent, as well." Abigail gushed.

"This is like old times," Annie said. "Only this time, I am actually interested in your love interest. Mr. Montgomery is quite the catch, Abigail. I only hope he knows what he is getting into."

"Ahem," the shopkeeper uttered, bringing Abigail down from the clouds.

"I suppose we should look at some fabric," Abigail said, patting Annie's shoulder, "Where can my friend freshen up?"

"Victoria, take the young lady to the back room."

Victoria curtsied to the shopkeeper. "Yes, ma'am." She led Annie to a white pitcher and washbowl decorated with a pink flower motif. Victoria looked over Annie's shoulder.

While Annie poured water into the bowl, she said, "I am quite capable of washing myself."

The shop girl left in a huff while Annie washed her face and hands. At the last second, she reached under her shirt and dabbed at her armpits.

Abigail delighted in the results when Annie returned from the back room. "You look almost presentable."

After taking Annie's measurements, the shopkeeper showed her fabrics of varying textures and color. Overwhelmed with the numerous selections, Annie finally made her decision. "White," she said.

Abigail could not contain her frustration with Annie. "White? There are reds and blues, greens and bold prints. Why would you choose a color so boring as white?"

"I disagree," the shopkeeper said. "A white dress will be a lovely contrast with the young lady's complexion. I can show her some lovely silk brocades."

Annie could not help but grin. "See, Abigail, I know all about fashion."

Lost in thought, the shopkeeper stood back, her finger tapping her right cheek as she studied Annie. "A blue embroidered stomacher will bring out the color in your eyes. You will look absolutely stunning." She then mumbled to herself, "Lace on the shift, a low-cut bodice on the dress. Perfect."

Once Annie and the shopkeeper agreed on the fabric, Christine tallied the cost.

"My friend will need the dress by this afternoon," Abigail said.

"Impossible," the shopkeeper said. "The earliest will

be sometime next week,"

"That is completely unacceptable." Abigail scanned the empty shop. "You don't appear busy."

"Wednesdays are our slow days. However, we have orders ahead of your friend's. And as you can see, I have a small staff."

Abigail opened the captain's drawstring purse, took out four gold coins and laid them on the counter in a straight line. "I am certain you will have it ready this afternoon. And if we are completely satisfied with the dress, I will give you and your girls each another gold coin."

Annie thought the shopkeeper's eyes were going to pop right out of her head.

"Milady is indeed generous!" she exclaimed.

"No, Captain Hawke is indeed generous," Annie said.

"Yes, we can have the dress ready by this afternoon. I won't be able to have any embroidery done on the stomacher, however. But I can add some nice beading to it."

Abigail laid another gold coin on the counter. "I am confident you can provide my friend with undergarments."

"By all means, and the young lady will need shoes. There is a cobbler two blocks away, just south of us," the shopkeeper said. She clapped her hands at the shop girls. "Victoria, Christine, we have work to do!"

Abigail glanced out the window. "I wonder what Mr. Montgomery and Robert are chatting about."

"They are probably talking about you, Abigail. I cannot think of a more fascinating subject. Can you?"

Abigail flashed a smile at Annie. "A more fascinating subject than me? Of course, not."

Annie chuckled. "You have not changed one bit since I have been gone."

"But you certainly have," Abigail said. "I cannot wait to get you out of those ugly clothes"

"I like these clothes," Annie said. She watched Abigail's eyebrow jut upward just like she had seen Captain Hawke's do so many times before. Hers, Annie thought, is annoying while the captain's is intriguing.

CHAPTER FORTY-FOUR

"What an exciting day this has been," Abigail said to Annie while the carriage bounced on the cobble stone street.

Annie ran her finger along the curved heel of a silk brocade shoe she held on her lap. "Exciting for you, not so much for me," she said. "Do I really have to wear these? They are terribly uncomfortable."

"Just be thankful the woman was late in returning for her shoes and the cobbler was easily bribed," Abigail said as she dangled Captain Hawke's drawstring purse in front of Annie's nose. "But you know I am not talking about our jaunt to the cobbler as being exciting. I am talking about our foray to Will's. What a splendid idea Mr. Montgomery had in suggesting we go to the coffeehouse in Covent Garden. All the times I have been to London and I didn't know a place like that existed."

Annie smiled. "Yes, Will's was quite an experience."

"It was so brave of you to bring me there," Abigail said to Mr. Montgomery.

"My pleasure," Mr. Montgomery replied. "I find it ridiculous that women are not allowed in coffeehouses. If women want to sip coffee while discussing politics or philosophy, then so be it."

Abigail fluttered her eyelashes at him. "You are such a rebel, Mr. Montgomery. And you Annie, what you said to that gentleman was priceless."

"His jaw dropped so low when he saw you walk in, Abigail, I had to say something." Annie dropped her voice. "You should close your mouth, sir, don't want to swallow a fly, now do we."

Mr. Montgomery roared with laughter. "I can assure you, they will be talking a long time about the lady who came to Will's."

"Little did they know you were accompanied by two ladies," Abigail said.

"No, Mr. Montgomery is correct," Annie said. "There was only one lady in Will's today."

Abigail patted Annie's hand. "We are having a good time today. We can have more days like this if you want to."

Annie was not willing to commit to anything more than: "Perhaps."

CHAPTER FORTY-FIVE

The shopkeeper greeted Annie back at the dress shop. "Hello, Miss Annie. Christine just finished sewing the blue panel to the bodice of your dress."

With the dress and undergarments draped over her arm, she led Annie to the dressing screen. "Victoria will assist you."

"That will not be necessary," Annie said.

"I am certain the young lady knows what she is doing," Abigail said.

"I would rather you join me."

"I would like that, too." Abigail turned to the shopkeeper. "Do you mind?"

The amiable shopkeeper simply smiled and nodded.

Annie disappeared with Abigail behind the screen. With her back to Abigail, she unbuttoned her shirt letting it fall to the floor. While her trousers rested on her hips, Annie revealed the faint scars traveling down her back. "I didn't wish to shock the girl," she said.

"You were ten when I first saw those scars, one of the times you stayed overnight. Do you remember I wanted to tell my parents, but you wouldn't let me. I should have told them. I will never forgive myself."

"You have no reason to feel guilty. You knew Aunt

Mary had threatened me, that if I told anyone, she would never let me see you again."

Abigail stroked Annie's arm. "You were afraid of never seeing me again. Why is it so different today?"

"Because today, I am not the same person. So much has happened."

When Annie looked away, Abigail sighed and grabbed the corset perched on a chair. "I know your scars don't hurt anymore, but this certainly will."

Annie raised her hands in lighthearted protest. "I refuse to wear that hideous thing."

"Oh, yes you will. All fashionable ladies wear them."

"I recall you calling them torture devises."

"They are," Abigail said cheerfully. "But if I must suffer, so will you. Now, let's get your shift on."

Annie pulled the knee-length undergarment, with lace at the neckline and at the bottom of its sleeves, over her head.

Abigail then wrapped the corset around Annie's waist and pulled the strings tight. "It's like old times, isn't it?"

"I'm suffocating." Annie's already small waistline became even smaller.

Abigail stepped back and admired her handiwork. "Look what you have been hiding under those dirty clothes of yours."

"My goodness!" Annie exclaimed as she looked down. Even she could appreciate the fuller breasts.

Abigail helped Annie with her petticoat. "Now the

most important part," Abigail said.

Like a cool breeze, the dress floated down over Annie's shoulders.

After she slipped each foot into her new shoes, Annie emerged cautiously from behind the screen. Taking wobbly steps in her new shoes, she turned in a circle showing off her dress to Mr. Montgomery, "What do you think, sir?"

While the bodice was not too revealing, Annie knew it dispelled any lingering doubts that Mr. Montgomery may have had about her.

"You are indeed a girl!" He exclaimed.

The shopkeeper stepped in front of Mr. Montgomery, directing Annie to a full-length mirror. "See for yourself what a lovely young woman you are."

Annie looked at herself from every angle. She touched the lace adorning the sleeves at the elbow. She then ran her fingers through her raven black hair and traced the line of her slender neck. When Annie caught everyone staring at her, she tugged on the sides of the dress. "It will do."

She then walked to the screen.

Abigail said, "Where are you going?"

"I must get my clothes."

"Victoria, already retrieved them for you," the shopkeeper said as she pointed to the counter where Annie's trousers and shirt, topped with her stockings, boots and Monmouth cap sat.

"Annie, why on earth do you want those ugly things?" Abigail asked.

"For when I return to the Realm."

"You cannot be serious." Abigail turned to Mr. Montgomery, "Talk some sense into her?"

"Give her time," he said.

Annie hugged the soiled clothes to her heart, remembering another shopping day, the one she went on with Christopher.

The bell jangled above the door one last time as Annie left for Spencer Estate.

CHAPTER FORTY-SIX

While her hand rested a breath away from Abigail's, Annie peered out the carriage window as the immaculate grounds of Spencer Estate passed by.

"You have barely spoken since we left London," Abigail said.

"You and Mr. Montgomery seem to have carried on quite well without me," Annie said looking at Mr. Montgomery sitting across from them.

Annie turned back to the carriage window and looked at the acres of breathtaking scenery, swans gliding on a lake, manicured shrubs, willow trees, horse paths and the stately three-story manor home up ahead.

"I almost forgot how beautiful it all is," she said.

"How does it compare to the ocean?" Abigail asked.

"The ocean has a beauty all its own," Annie said.

"I will take your word for it."

The four high-stepping horses clip clopped on the brick circle at the front of the manor house. The carriage barely rolled to a stop, when Annie bounded out. Assisted by Robert, Mr. Montgomery and Abigail stepped out of the carriage and quickly caught up with Annie on the lawn.

Unlike the Realm, where each day brought the

unexpected, time stood still at Spencer Estate. Beautiful, sedate, predictable, Annie thought.

She ran up the stone steps leading to the oak paneled door. Annie stepped aside for Abigail to bang the brass door knocker. And then came the wait.

The Spencer's butler, Gerard, appeared in the arched doorway looking as ancient as the Grecian urn that stood behind him. He mumbled something to Abigail after she introduced Mr. Montgomery to him. He then escorted her, Mr. Montgomery and Annie into the foyer.

"Annie, please show Mr. Montgomery our ancestral paintings while I go to the library to see Mother and Father."

"I am anxious to see them, Abigail."

"I know you are, but I need to talk to them first. Gerard told me they're upset with me," Abigail said.

"Nothing changes at Spencer Estate," Annie said.

Abigail set off for the library. Annie followed close behind while Mr. Montgomery yawned at a life-size painting hanging on the wall.

Standing just outside the library, Annie spied Abigail's parents surrounded by bookshelves rising to the ceiling. Lady Spencer, wearing a red dress with ruffled trumpet sleeves, appeared engrossed in her husband puffing on his clay pipe. He must be really upset, Annie thought, for Lady Spencer to allow him to smoke his pipe inside.

When Abigail entered, Lady Spencer sprung from her chair. The couple got halfway across the room, when Lady Spencer began scolding Abigail. "Do you know how worried your father and I have been?"

"Worried, about what, Mother?"

"As if you didn't know," Lady Spencer said as she fanned herself.

"The Cudney sisters told their parents about your London escapades," Lord Spencer said. "Lucky for us, they were quite put out that you didn't invite them along today. They said you were going to meet a *man*, a sailor, of all things!"

"Father, is that all they told you?"

"You mean there is more?" he said.

"Oh my, I need to sit down," Lady Spencer said as she made her way back to her chair with Abigail's help.

"I have been going to the London docks looking for Annie," Abigail said.

"Abigail, I know you miss the girl. We all do, but you must come to terms with the fact that she is gone, and you will never see her again."

"Mother, Annie is here."

"Here? She's here?" As if Annie would magically appear at her feet, Lady Spencer pointed down at the floor.

Abigail took her mother's hand and gestured toward the entry to the library.

Not certain what her reception would be, Annie walked slowly until she heard Lady Spencer gasp. "My prayers have been answered."

Annie kicked off her shoes and padded across the hardwood floor to Lady Spencer's waiting arms.

While they embraced each other tightly, Lord Spencer rubbed Annie's shoulders.

"I see you have done well for yourself," Lord Spencer said as he studied Annie's clothes.

"I have, but these clothes..."

Abigail broke in. "She was not wearing these clothes when I first found her. What a sight she was."

Not taking her eyes off Annie, Lady Spencer said. "What do you mean?"

"Yesterday, she was not wearing a dress."

Lord Spencer looked shocked. "You saw her yesterday in London and didn't tell us?"

"If Annie decided not to return with me, I didn't want to see your hopes dashed."

In a hushed tone, Lady Spencer inquired, "Annie, if you weren't wearing a dress yesterday, were you... naked?"

Annie knew she had better put Lady Spencer's mind at ease before the poor woman keeled over in a dead faint. "Trousers," Annie said. "I was wearing trousers."

Seeing the shocked expression on Lady Spencer's face, Annie wondered if wearing trousers, wasn't much better than being naked.

"Yesterday," Abigail said. "She looked like a street urchin."

"I strongly disagree, Abigail. I looked like a sailor."

Lady Spencer responded with a moan.

When Annie saw Gerard accompany Mr. Montgomery into the library, she hoped the pressure would be taken off her.

Gerard cleared his throat and announced, "Mr. Matthew Montgomery."

"And who exactly are you?" Lord Spencer said.

Before Mr. Montgomery could say anything, Abigail attempted to explain. "Father, this is the gentleman who accompanied Annie when I found her at the docks. He is the first mate on the merchant ship, the Realm. Yesterday, he and Annie needed to attend to some unpleasant business. A young man had met an untimely death aboard the ship and they had to tell his mother."

"Dreadful," Lady Spencer said from her chair. "Simply dreadful."

Lord Spencer looked at Annie. "If I am hearing this correctly, you have been living your life as a sailor. How can that be?"

"It is a long story."

"I have all day," Lord Spencer said before he turned to Abigail. "And you, young lady, I will deal with you later."

Abigail and Mr. Montgomery slipped out of the library as Lord Spencer settled in a chair next to his wife and told Annie to do the same.

Annie's questioning began. While Lord and Lady Spencer had learned from Annie's cousin Erik that she had run away to London, that was all they knew. Annie filled in the blanks for them.

Seeing how Lady Spencer reacted when Annie told them she had begged on the streets, she decided to leave out certain parts about her time on the Realm. From Lord Spencer's expressions Annie realized that he knew she was leaving out details. His wife, however, looked contented with Annie's abridged version of her time on the streets, the Realm and her endeavors with her shipmates.

It was Lord Spencer's turn to inform Annie of how a week had passed before any of the Spencer's knew she was even missing. Erik had told them that Annie needed time to grieve her uncle's death. He had done exactly what she had told him to do, Annie thought to herself. By the time a search party was sent to London, it was too late.

"You made the best of a most difficult situation, Annie," Lord Spencer said. "I only wish you had come to us. We never would have allowed anything bad to happen to you if we had only known. Your Aunt Mary is gone and she can never harm you again."

"Abigail told me you made certain she would never return. Thank you, sir."

"You need to spend time with Abigail. Since your disappearance, she has been more short-tempered than usual. She has missed you terribly. We all have."

"Now where do you suppose that girl has run off to?" Lady Spencer said.

"She probably took Mr. Montgomery for a stroll in the garden," Annie said.

"It will be dark soon. That girl is going to be the death of me," Lady Spencer said.

"You have nothing to worry about, ma'am. I can

assure you, Mr. Montgomery is a man of good character. In fact, he is the son of Roger Montgomery, the Earl of Leeds."

Lord Spencer muttered under his breath, "He is, undoubtedly, Roger's wayward son."

CHAPTER FORTY-SEVEN

The back entrance opened to a garden of mature trees. The scent of roses filled the air. No longer wearing her shoes, Annie, discarded her stockings, as well, before going off the stone path. She felt the fertile soil squeeze between her toes.

Hidden among the foliage and deepening shadows, Annie found Mr. Montgomery and Abigail making polite conversation. He pushed her on a swing hanging from an oak branch while Abigail sniffed the fragrance of a freshly picked rose in her hand.

"And exactly what does a first mate do?" Annie heard Abigail ask.

She tiptoed closer, straining to hear every word.

"I work more closely with the men than the captain does. And if he should become ill, or die, God forbid, I take command of the ship." Mr. Montgomery said.

"Fascinating," she said. "Now kiss me, Mr. Montgomery."

"I assume you mean your hand, milady."

"You assume wrong, Mr. Montgomery." She closed her eyes.

Annie anxiously waited for Mr. Montgomery to make his move. Inching forward to get a better view, she grabbed hold of a drooping branch. When it snapped off in her hand, it got Mr. Montgomery's attention. He spun around, and in two leaps caught Annie before she hit the ground.

With Annie nestled in his arms, he sheepishly said to Abigail, "Force of habit!"

"I am supposed to be in your arms, not her!" Abigail tapped her foot. "How long have you been watching us, Annie?"

"Long enough." Annie looked up at Mr. Montgomery. "She fancies you, sir, but be forewarned, she is a handful."

"I will take note of that," he replied.

* * *

Candles flickered above the dining room table from two cut-glass chandeliers.

No sooner had Annie sat next to Abigail, she heard footsteps echoing on the hardwood floor. Twisting his cap in his hands, a teenage boy appeared in the dining room. He looked toward Lord Spencer. "Robert said you wished to see me, sir."

Appearing uncomfortable, the youth checked out his surroundings. Annie could barely contain herself while she observed him taking in the ornate furniture and embroidered drapery. Then his eyes met hers.

"Annie? Annie!" he said.

"Erik!" Annie jumped to her feet and raced to him.

He grabbed her by the waist and twirled her in the air. Just as quickly, he gently put her down as if he was afraid she would break. "My, my, you are a lot prettier than I last saw you. And, I hate to admit it, but you actually look like a lady."

She ruffled his red hair. "And you are as handsome as ever, Erik Moore."

He clutched Annie's hand so tight her fingers hurt. "I never thought you would return. Did you make it to London?" he asked.

"Aye."

"Aye, you say. You made it to the sea, didn't you?" He laughed as he slapped his cap across his knee. "If you met up with any pirates, I hope it wasn't in that dress!"

"Oh Erik, I have so much to tell you!"

Gerard moved from the arched doorway to Erik's side and cleared his throat.

"I think he wants us to sit," Annie said.

Erik murmured. "Here? I'm rather dusty." He confirmed that fact by smacking his cap against his trousers once more.

"Erik, for heaven's sake, sit!" Lord Spencer ordered.

Erik thumped Gerard on the back before draping his arm around Annie's shoulder. Once he took his place across from Annie, a tureen of soup was served. Lord Spencer made a toast to everyone's health and to their good fortune in having Annie back in their lives. Mr. Montgomery followed with a toast to the family's kind generosity.

"I will drink to that," Erik said.

Halfway through the first course of goose, rabbit, and fresh fruits, Annie wondered if her stomach would burst. After the eating utensils and tablecloth were replaced with new ones, she could only look at the second course placed on the table.

"Annie, aren't you hungry?" Lady Spencer said.

"Everything is quite wonderful. But after hardtack and salt pork, I am not used to such rich food."

"Oh, my," Lady Spencer said.

Unlike Annie, Erik barely took time to breathe as he shoveled each portion into his mouth.

The meal concluded with fruits, small cakes, jellies and cream. Lord Spencer and Mr. Montgomery enjoyed a glass of Taylor's Port while Lady Spencer sipped sweet wine.

A manservant behind Annie placed a trifle in front of her. She gazed at the layers of cake, fruit, custard and cream. "You remembered."

"How could we forget?" Lord Spencer said.

Lady Spencer smiled at Mr. Montgomery. "That was the first dessert Annie had in our home. When I heard that her aunt and uncle had taken her in after her parents had died, I told Benjamin we must have that child over for some sweets. To think that was eight years ago—seems like yesterday."

Lord Spencer looked fondly at Annie. "You stole our hearts from the moment you stepped out of the carriage. I still remember that awkward curtsy of yours."

"Aunt Mary made me practice it all night."

Lady Spencer's eyes welled up with tears. "Annie, you were simply enchanting. When I saw you, I knew immediately that you would be a perfect companion for our daughter. She had scared off all her other playmates."

"Being I was so young, you must have had some doubts I could do the job," Annie said.

"Never. Despite your gentle manner and tender age, I knew you would be able to hold your own with our arrogant daughter."

"Mother, please, Mr. Montgomery must think I am a monster."

He laughed. "Headstrong, perhaps, but I could never think of you as a monster."

Annie took two bites of the dessert. She licked the cream from her lips before putting her fork down.

"Is the trifle not prepared properly?" Lord Spencer asked.

"Oh, no, it is perfect in every way, but I simply don't have much of an appetite.

"How can I ever thank you for being so kind? I feel as though I never left." Annie saw jubilation flash across Abigail's face.

Annie pushed her chair away from the table. "May I please be excused?"

"Certainly, you have had quite an exhausting day," Lord Spencer said. He turned to Abigail. "Go with your mother to the drawing room while Mr. Montgomery and I retire to the study. Erik, I assume you must have some work to do at the stable."

"Yes, sir. But if you don't mind, I will take these fine vittles back with me. We don't want 'em to go to waste, now do we." Erik scraped his food onto a delicately embroidered napkin. "Don't worry, sir, I will bring your napkin back as good as new."

"That won't be necessary," Lord Spencer said.

Annie hugged Erik before she hastened upstairs to Abigail's bedroom.

* * *

Annie plopped herself down, lightly bouncing on Abigail's bed. She moved aside a glass-eyed doll before resting back on the plump pillow. So soft, certainly more comfortable than my hammock, she thought.

Annie sniffed the air. Abigail's room smelled of fresh lilac. Nothing smelled musty or damp. Scents, Annie realized she missed.

"Are you alright?" Abigail asked as she entered the room.

"I just needed some time alone."

"I understand, but now that you are back, I don't want you out of my sight even for a minute. It will be like old times. Remember how we used to comb out each other's hair?"

Annie ran her fingers through her short locks. "Not quite like old times."

"It will grow out."

"Maybe," Annie said, "I don't want it to."

CHAPTER FORTY-EIGHT

Three weeks had passed since Annie arrived at Spencer Estate. She watched as Erik saddled her favorite chestnut mare.

"I have seen you or Anthony saddle Chelsea a hundred times. I am certain I can do it myself," Annie said.

Abigail sat tall on her black gelding. "You don't ride side saddle anymore and I let you wear trousers when we ride together, but I put my foot down when it comes to saddling your own horse, Annie. There are just some things ladies simply do not do,"

Abigail turned to Annie's cousin. "Erik, hurry up. Robert has a picnic waiting for us at the lake."

"Maybe you should be wearing the trousers," Erik said under his breath.

"I heard that, Erik," Abigail said. "Annie, your cousin needs to mind his tongue."

Annie grinned at Erik. "Mind your tongue."

As hard as she tried, Abigail couldn't keep from laughing. "One Moore is bad enough, but two are impossible."

Annie reached into the stall where Lord Spencer's blood bay Thoroughbred stood. Standing sixteen hands tall with a white star in the middle of his forehead, the magnificent steed nuzzled Annie's closed hand.

"Miss Annie, if you are thinking 'bout asking me if you can ride him, my answer will always be the same: No," Anthony, said.

Annie opened her hand revealing a carrot. "Why not? Lord Spencer seldom rides him," Annie said to the dark-haired groom.

"I do as I am told which is what you should do. I keep Phantom exercised. He is always ready for a good run, but he is too much horse for you, Annie."

"But he likes me. See?" Annie rubbed Phantom's nose while he chomped on the carrot.

"Everyone likes you, Annie, but when it comes to you riding Phantom, the answer will always be the same," Anthony said as he handed Erik a shovel to clean the stalls.

Grudgingly, Annie mounted Chelsea.

* * *

That evening, Annie and Abigail took turns reading Shakespeare sonnets to each other. When their eyes became heavy, they closed the book and reclined on their pillows.

They talked about every topic except one, Annie's experiences on the Realm. When Annie tried, Abigail would place the back of her hand across her pale forehead, grab her silver pomander containing smelling salts and say, "Oh, please, Annie, your stories will surely give me the vapors."

However, one resident of the Realm remained a

popular subject, Mr. Montgomery. "I cannot wait for tomorrow. Do you think Matthew is as excited about seeing me as I am about seeing him?"

"I am certain he has thought of nothing else. After all, he has visited you almost every day since I arrived here," Annie said.

"He writes me the sweetest notes," Abigail said as she pulled one out from under her pillow. She clutched it to her heart.

"I am anxious for tomorrow evening as well. I cannot wait to see Doc and Captain Hawke. Did you know this will be the first time in over three years that Doc has stepped off the Realm?"

"He must be quite fond of you, Annie." With a sly grin on her lips, Abigail said, "I am curious. Did you ever think of any of the men on the Realm in a romantic sort of way?"

"I thought you didn't want me to talk about the Realm."

"I don't, but I am curious about the men. So answer the question. Did you have any romantic interests?"

"Certainly not. Such thoughts would have been too dangerous."

"As Shakespeare once wrote, 'the lady doth protest too much.' Annie, you are not fooling me. You are trying so hard not to smile. Someone did catch your eye. Who is he?"

Annie thought a moment. "Ambrose Barrette."

"Tell me more."

"There isn't much to tell, but Barrette is mighty fine

looking, black hair past his shoulders, the darkest eyes. Not as dark as Captain Hawke's eyes, mind you, but dark nevertheless." Annie smiled up at the canopy. "If I tell you anymore, you might get the vapors."

"If something scandalous happened, I want to hear all about it."

"I saw Barrette without his shirt on."

Abigail's eyes widened. "Oh my, now that is scandalous!"

Annie enjoyed Abigail being interested in *her* love life for a change, even if she didn't really have one.

"However, since he thought I was a boy, it wasn't all that scandalous. Besides, he was only changing his shirt. But then again, Doc had a feeling..." Annie giggled.

"Don't stop there," Abigail said.

"It is just silly."

"I do not care if it is silly or not. I want to know what Doc said."

"Alright, I'll tell you. Doc said Barrette didn't look at me the way a sailor looks at another sailor. I told him it was just his imagination, but once when Barrette and I were alone in the fo'c'sle, he started to brush a strand of hair from my face and I saw that look. At least, I thought I did. Anyway, it gave me goose bumps."

"Annie, you are beginning to sound more like a girl every day."

"But seriously, Abigail, since I've been here, I realize that Barrette is nothing more than an amusing *and* annoying friend."

"A friend who just happens to be mighty fine looking, especially without his shirt on," Abigail reminded Annie. "Is this Barrette fellow better looking than Mr. Montgomery?"

"It is impossible to compare the two." Annie said. "And while Mr. Montgomery is indeed a handsome bloke, I look at him the same way you look at your brothers."

"What about Doc?"

"That's easy. I see him as my father. And I say that with all due respect to my real father. He would have loved Doc as much as I do."

"I remember you saying something about Captain Hawke dresses like a drunken toad. I'm curious. What does he look like?"

"Oh my, there is no describing the captain," Annie said.

"What do you mean?"

"He is like no other."

"Is he handsome?"

"I will let you be the judge of that when you meet him."

"Oh, I understand. You are being diplomatic. Captain Hawke is a craggy old man, doesn't have all his teeth, and he's bald."

Annie laughed. "I could not have described him any better than if he were standing in this room.

"Abigail, I always wondered how jealous you would be if you knew I was in the middle of the ocean surrounded by all these men. You have always been such a flirt."

"Not anymore since Matthew came into my life." Abigail looked dreamily off in space. "I cannot wait for tomorrow."

"Neither can I. I must tell the captain what I have decided." Annie extinguished the candle on the bed stand. "Good night, Abigail."

"Good night, Annie."

CHAPTER FORTY-NINE

With her feet dangling over the edge of the canopy bed, Annie watched Abigail admire herself in the freestanding mirror. She wondered how one person could stare at herself for so long and not be bored.

"How do I look?" Abigail asked.

Annie assessed Abigail's lavender silk brocade gown accented with gold thread. "You needn't wear such a fancy dress to impress Mr. Montgomery," she answered.

"I shall do whatever it takes to win Matthew's heart."

"I think you have already done that. But remember, he is a sailor, a man whose first love will always be the sea," Annie said as she slid off the bed.

"I am certain I have made dry land most appealing to him," Abigail said as she pinched her cheeks until they glowed a rosy pink.

Annie nudged Abigail out of the way and stared at her own image in the mirror. "Sometimes I wonder who this stranger is. I barely recognize her. What do you suppose the captain will think when he sees me?"

"I will tell you one thing, Annie, he won't see that little street urchin he hired as his cabin boy anymore."

"Really?" Annie said.

"Oh please, Annie, don't you have any idea how lovely you are?"

Annie continued to stare at the mirror. "Me? Lovely?"

"You little scamp. I see that grin," Abigail said as she grabbed Annie's hand. "It is time to go downstairs and wait for our guests."

* * *

It was dusk when Gerard announced, "Mr. Matthew Montgomery and Doctor Arthur Cromwell."

"Doc!"

Annie ran to greet him. She threw her arms around his thick waist. Her head rested a moment on his chest before she touched his deeply lined face. Gone was his grey stubble, but his bushy mustache remained intact as did his furrowed brow. "You look positively dashing, Doc." she said.

He patted Annie's hand. "My goodness, Mr. Montgomery was right. He said you were as lovely as an Arabian princess."

"She certainly is," Lord Spencer said as he welcomed his arriving guests.

Annie peered around Mr. Montgomery. "The captain, is he still in the carriage?"

"Captain Hawke has been delayed."

"I understand he is at the Hollingsworth Estate," Lord Spencer said. "I assume he is conducting business with Samuel."

Terrence Cudney, a long-time friend of Lord Spencer, asked, "Is it true Hollingsworth exports all of his wool to the American colonies on the Realm?"

"You are quite correct, sir, but Captain Hawke's visit is more pleasure than business," Mr. Montgomery answered.

* * *

Lord Spencer escorted Terrence's wife into the dining room where Lady Spencer had already taken her place at the head of the table. The Cudney sisters, Catherine and Hannah, quickly found their places on either side of their mother. Mr. Montgomery needed no prompting to sit across from Abigail while Annie stared at the empty chair between him and Doc. She slipped off her shoes and wiggled her sore toes under the table.

Once the first course was over, servants replaced the linen tablecloth, plates and eating utensils with clean ones. An hour into the second course, Annie sat straighter in her chair when she heard the door knocker banging in the foyer. She listened with excited anticipation to the firm boot heels drowning out the butler's shuffling footsteps.

Gerard escorted the guest into the dining room. "Captain Jonathan Hawke," he announced.

As the captain strutted into the dining room, more than one eyebrow peaked, and all were female.

Lord Spencer rose from his chair. "I am delighted you could join us, Captain Hawke."

The captain appeared elegant in a well-tailored blue waistcoat as he greeted each dinner guest he was introduced him to. His swarthy complexion and tangled black hair were in sharp contrast to his shirt's delicate ruffled collar and cuffs. Certain he had raided Mr. Montgomery's wardrobe, Annie could not help but smile.

Hannah and Catherine showed their approval of the captain with eyes glazed over.

Abigail whispered to Annie, "He certainly is not dressed like a drunken toad, and I was expecting someone much older. That is one wickedly handsome man."

Annie whispered back, "I thought it was amusing when you said what you thought he would look like. You know he's not much older than Mr. Montgomery."

Abigail playfully nudged Annie's arm as they giggled together.

"And, of course, you know Annie," Lord Spencer said. "I can't imagine what she and my daughter have found so amusing."

The captain's rigid jaw and stern eyes softened. "Annie and I have met a time or two."

In her white dress, and silk stocking feet, Annie got up from her chair. She twisted a short strand of dark hair between her fingertips. "This is the dress you bought me, Captain. Do you like it?" she shyly asked.

He gestured for Annie to turn in a circle. The dress revealed a young lady who was no longer a child, but not quite a woman. Mr. Montgomery broke the awkward silence. "I believe she looks like an Arabian princess. What are your thoughts, Jonathan?"

No one said a word as the captain studied Annie as

if she were storm clouds brewing off a ship's bow. Breathless, Annie awaited the verdict.

"I do not agree with Mr. Montgomery," he finally said. "Annie most certainly does not look like an Arabian princess."

While Hannah and Catherine tittered, Annie put on a brave face, but she knew her red cheeks had given away her humiliation.

Captain Hawke stepped around to the other side of the table. As he cupped Annie's chin in his hand, he gazed down on her with brooding eyes. "When you are an angel, how could you possibly look like an earthly princess?"

The Cudney sisters stopped their snickering and uttered a collective sigh.

After the captain took his seat between Doc and Mr. Montgomery, Abigail asked him, "I am curious, Captain. Will you be returning to the Hollingsworth Estate or going back to the ship?"

"To the ship. Why do you ask?"

"I thought perhaps you fancy Charlotte Hollingsworth. I have not seen her in a while, but I remember her as being rather attractive. Although, I wish she would do something with that dreadful hair of hers. Is there any possibility she will become Mrs. Hawke?"

Abigail's question sent Annie plummeting back to earth.

Lord Spencer looked shocked. "What in the world has gotten into you, Abigail? Show the captain some respect."

"It is quite alright. I find curious women intriguing," the captain said.

With a smile and one slightly raised eyebrow, he looked back at Abigail. "Charlotte is a lovely young woman, but I believe her fiancée, Percy Brighton, would object to her becoming my wife. I am surprised you were not aware of Charlotte's engagement."

Hannah's head bobbed up and down. "I knew that," she said.

"Me, too," her sister concurred.

"I have not seen Charlotte or her family for some time," Abigail said. "How do you know The Hollingsworth's, Captain Hawke? You obviously have more than a business relationship with their family."

"I became acquainted with them about three years ago when they were on the Godspeed. They had been guests of Captain Everett," Captain Hawke said.

"I remember Charlotte telling me of her family's plight on that ill-fated ship. An interesting tale, but I believed little of it, especially the part about a gallant pirate."

"I remember you telling me the story," Annie said. "But I thought you believed it."

"I believed it up to a point, but it never could have been Godenot's ship that overtook the Godspeed. Even at age fourteen, I knew his reputation. There would have been no survivors and a gallant pirate is a contradiction in terms," Abigail replied.

"So you dismissed the story as nothing more than a

fairy tale?" Captain Hawke said.

Abigail brought her gold fork to her mouth and paused. "I most certainly did. And what were you on The Godspeed, Captain Hawke, a guest or a deckhand?"

The captain twisted the end of his thin mustache. "Neither—I was the gallant pirate."

CHAPTER FIFTY

Captain Hawke's admission and Abigail's clanging fork brought all eating to a standstill. A manservant dashed to catch her utensil in mid-bounce as it ricocheted off the edge of her plate.

Mr. Montgomery surveyed the faces of the stunned dinner guests. "Well, Jonathan, you certainly know how to liven up an evening."

Captain Hawke pulled out his Spanish dagger, speared a duck breast and plopped it onto his plate. "They must have missed the part about my being a *gallant* pirate."

Annie could not hide her disgust. "If you were one of Godenot's men, there would have been nothing gallant about you."

As Annie and Captain Hawke faced off, the mood at the table became tense.

"You don't understand," Captain Hawke said.

"What is there to understand? Have you forgotten I boarded the Margaret Louise? I know firsthand what Godenot's men are capable of doing. It was a ghost ship. Palmer lost his father because of those pirates, because of men like you."

Ready to flee, Annie rose from her chair. Mr. Montgomery jumped up at the same time.

"Annie, the captain is right. You don't understand," he said.

"We are not talking about just any pirate, Mr. Montgomery. He was one of Godenot's men. How can you defend him? You were on the Margaret Louise with me."

"Yes, but I also was on the Godspeed," Mr. Montgomery said.

"You were on the Godspeed?" Annie turned from Mr. Montgomery to Captain Hawke. "Is that when you saved Mr. Montgomery's life for the second time?"

"Aye, and truth be told, I saved the whole bloody ship."

Annie sat back down. "The whole bloody ship, you say."

Lady Spencer wagged her finger at Annie. "Young lady, watch your tongue."

"Watch your tongue?" Lord Spencer said. "Good grief, woman, is that all you can say after witnessing what has to be the most interesting conversation we have ever had in this dining room?"

If Lord Spencer had sat any closer to the edge of his chair, he would have fallen off. "How could one man, a pirate at that, rescue an entire ship?" He asked the captain.

Captain Hawke held up his hand with his thumb and index finger almost touching. "I may have exaggerated just a bit, sir."

"You are too modest, Jonathan," Mr. Montgomery said as he stabbed at an unseen adversary with his fork. "One moment I am at the helm and the next moment, I am crossing swords with pirates. If Jonathan had not been on our side, those of us on the Godspeed would be nothing more than a memory today."

"Please, I wish to hear more," Lord Spencer said. "If you ladies want to leave, please feel free to do so."

"I would not miss this for the world," Abigail replied.

The two Cudney sisters continued fanning their mother. No one exited the dining room.

Captain Hawke looked at Annie across the table. "Yes, I was a pirate on the Crimson Revenge, but not by choice. Mr. Allan and I..."

Annie looked dumbfounded. "Mr. Allan was a pirate? But he is such a gentle soul."

"Annie, I will try to answer all your questions, but for now, please just listen," the captain said. "As I was saying, Mr. Allan and I were shipmates on the Eden Castle when we were attacked by the Crimson Revenge. After our shipmates, for lack of a better way of putting it, were disposed of; Godenot took us and four other bosuns captive. Mr. Allan and I are the only ones who survived. I will spare you the unpleasant details. Mr. Allan and I promised each other that we would do whatever it took to stay alive...and escape.

"After two months, Mr. Allan and I won Godenot's confidence to board a captured ship. What he didn't know, is that five of his pirates agreed to mutiny with us. Their hatred for Godenot far outweighed their fear of him. After the Crimson Revenge fired cannons across the Godspeed's bow, I knew I had to implement my plan or all would be lost." Captain Hawke took a sip of his brandy.

Mr. Montgomery took over. "Even though it had been some ten years since I had last seen Jonathan," Mr. Montgomery said. "I would have recognized him anywhere. His swagger alone would have been hard to forget. When I realized he was on our side, it gave me hope. He had placed his mutineers strategically on the Godspeed, including himself at the bow and Mr. Allan aft."

The captain jumped back into the story. "But if the Godspeed crew hadn't joined in the fight, my plan never would have succeeded. They fought valiantly. Young and old spilt their blood that day. They had nothing to lose.

"Godenot expected little opposition and none from his own crew. Once the fighting began, four more pirates took our side." He looked at Abigail. "Matthew is a fine swordsman, a brave man. He can have my back any day."

"Captain, I should never have doubted you," Annie said.

"What else were you to think?"

"I suppose, but Captain, I am curious."

Captain Hawke smiled. "Why does that not surprise me?"

"Are there any other pirates now on the Realm besides Mr. Allan?"

"Former pirates," he said.

"I stand corrected," Annie said.

"Would you care to guess?"

"Symington." Who else, Annie thought.

The captain laughed. "Ah, the obvious choice, but no, not Symington. He was the Godspeed's carpenter and Mr. Waverly, their cook. However, Ainsworth was one of Godenot's pirates, as were three of my gunners."

"What became of the Godspeed's captain?" Annie asked.

"Godenot is a cunning fiend. With the sun blinding Everette's eyes, the poor man didn't stand a chance. Before the pirates retreated, Godenot ran Captain Everette through with his sword," Captain Hawke said.

The grisly detail made Lady Cudney's eyes roll back in her head. The Cudney sisters fanned her even faster.

"I knew the Godspeed couldn't outmaneuver the Crimson Revenge and they had no cannons, but we had to try," Captain Hawke said. "But to our relief, Godenot's ship changed course and sailed away."

"Surely, they were more than capable of blowing The Godspeed out of the water," Annie said. "Why didn't they?"

"That is a question I have often asked myself. I will never forget Godenot looking at me from the deck of the Crimson Revenge. God be my witness, he smiled a dead man's smile at me. He will seek his revenge when I least expect it."

As if he had been crossing swords with the pirates himself, Lord Spencer caught his breath. "Quite a tale, gentlemen. Would you care for some more brandy? I know I could use a glass or two."

As the discussion turned to lighter matters of business and politics, the ladies stood to retire to the drawing room with Lady Spencer leading the way.

"Sir, do you mind if Annie joins me in the parlor? I have some business I wish to discuss with her," Captain Hawke said.

"Certainly, Captain, take all the time you need."

In the parlor, Captain Hawke pulled up an Italian walnut armchair across from Annie. "The Realm will be sailing soon," he said.

"I know and I have made up my mind."

He cut her off, "Arrangements have been made for you to stay here."

Annie's mouth dropped open. "What do you mean arrangements have been made? I thought this was my decision to make."

"After spending three weeks with the Spencer's, I thought this would be your decision. Look at you, Annie. You are a young lady, not a sailor." He reached for her hands, but she would have none of it. "The Spencer's can give you much more than you can possibly have on the Realm. In fact, Mr. Montgomery believes they wish to adopt you," he said

Annie felt her lungs constrict. "Adopt me?"

"Would that be so terrible? They consider you one of their own. Annie, think of it, everything you ever dreamed of is yours for the asking: beautiful clothes, tutored in every subject, courted by the finest gentlemen."

"Do you not know me? Those are not my dreams. I am Annie Moore, a fisherman's daughter, not a Spencer, nor do I want to be."

"Aha, you said you are Annie Moore, not Andrés de la Cruz. Whether you realize it or not, you know exactly who you are. It is settled. When the Realm sets sail, you will not be on her."

"I do know who I am, and it will be Annie Moore who returns to the Realm, not Andrés de la Cruz. I earned the respect of my shipmates, and I can do it again."

"You will not return to the Realm and that is final."

Annie felt the walls closing in on her. Lost in her anger, she didn't hear Abigail and Mr. Montgomery enter the parlor.

"May we join you?" Abigail asked.

Annie dug her nails into the floral-print upholstery and glared at her.

Captain Hawke stood up. "Matthew, Abigail, take good care of Annie."

Without another word, Captain Hawke retreated to the hall. He didn't look back.

Abigail placed her hand on Annie's shoulder, but Annie shrugged it off.

She got up from the chair, and screamed at them, "Neither of you ever asked me what I had decided about returning to the Realm. Now, I know why. The decision had been made for me. You all conspired against me."

Darting into the hall, she called to Captain Hawke, "I'm a Jack-tar and don't you ever forget it."

Mr. Montgomery ran after her and pulled Annie back into the parlor. She lashed out at him with her free hand. He in turn grabbed both wrists, but not before Annie drew blood. She whipped about in his arms until there was no fight left in her.

Abigail rushed to Mr. Montgomery's side. "Matthew, your cheek!"

"It is only a scratch," he assured her.

While Abigail dabbed at the scratch with a handkerchief, she turned to Annie, "We only have your best interests in mind."

Annie sank into the armchair, drawing her knees to her chest. "Why does everyone think they know what is best for me?"

Huffing and puffing, Doc appeared in the doorway. "Jonathan left without so much as a goodbye and Lord Spencer dismissed all the commotion we heard as nothing to worry about."

He looked at Mr. Montgomery's face. "What happened to you? Let me take a look."

Mr. Montgomery waved him off. "It's just a scratch," Mr. Montgomery said.

"Oh, Annie, your beautiful dress is ripped." Doc said. "What is going on in here?

"We are all fine, Doc, just clumsy," she said.

Doc muttered. "Too much excitement, I should never have left the ship."

Annie rushed to guide Doc to a chair. She forced a

smile. "You needn't fret, Doc. Once you are back on the Realm, you can get a good night's sleep."

"Yes," Abigail said, patting Doc's slumped shoulder. "I will have Robert summon a carriage for you."

Annie led Doc into the hall and looked over her shoulder. "Abigail, I'll get Robert and then I'll be off to my room. Will you be joining me?"

Abigail whispered to Mr. Montgomery, but not soft enough for Annie not to hear. "She seems to be coming around faster than I thought she would."

"Too quick, if you ask me," Mr. Montgomery replied.

CHAPTER FIFTY-ONE

Annie sat on the edge of the bed. "You were right, Abigail. This is where I belong. I will miss the Realm..."

She turned away, and wiped her eyes.

Abigail placed her hands on her hips. "I always knew you would come to your senses, but I did not expect it to happen this soon. I am not sure I believe you."

Annie continued to dab at her eyes with a handkerchief. "I will miss my shipmates terribly, but you have always known me to be a practical person. What would be more practical than living here? Look around, Abigail. Anyone would be foolish to give up all of this. Could you?"

"Certainly not," Abigail said.

"I think I have always known I belonged here, but I had been too stubborn to admit it." Annie sniffed and blew her nose. "I'm sorry, Abigail, but I won't be much company this evening. Why don't you sit in the parlor with Mr. Montgomery. When the fire burns out, you can snuggle real close to him. I am certain he will want to keep you warm."

Abigail sighed. "How romantic, I will be certain to have Mother and Father retire early."

Annie followed Abigail to the door and waved to her as she descended the staircase. Annie called after her, "Good night, Abigail."

"Good night, Annie."

Once Abigail was out of sight, Annie rushed to the wardrobe. She searched for her clothes from the ship.

After changing into her sailor's attire, Annie began composing a letter.

My dearest Abigail,

With pen in hand, I write with heavy heart. Had I known your parents would have taken me in, I might never have left. But I did leave and I found another world. I do not expect you to understand. The Realm is where I truly belong. Once I have returned, the captain will realize he was wrong. You will always be my dearest friend. Never forget that. Give my love to your kind parents and Erik. I will see you all again. I promise.

After signing it, Annie stood in the darkened doorway. Assured she neither saw nor heard anyone coming down the hall, she tiptoed out of the bedroom and down the stairs. She heard laughter and talking coming from the parlor. Annie couldn't make out what they were saying, but hoped she was the last thing on Abigail and Mr. Montgomery's minds.

CHAPTER FIFTY-TWO

With the reins looped over her arm, Annie stroked the high-spirited stallion's forelock. "Good boy," she said while she awkwardly fastened the bridle. "Anthony can't stop me from riding you this time."

Having watched Chelsea saddled dozens of times, Annie believed saddling Phantom should be easy. Standing on a stool, Annie threw a blanket slightly past the blood bay's withers. She spoke softly trying not to spook him.

After cinching the saddle, she waited a moment for Phantom to relax. "Now the hard part," she said while she wiped her sweaty palms on her trousers. Annie cinched the saddle even tighter. Phantom snorted. She wondered if he was voicing his impatience with her. "Sorry if I am a little slow at this, but I haven't had much practice."

The stool wobbled as she pulled herself onto the saddle. Phantom stomped the ground. They were both anxious to leave the stable.

With any luck, Annie thought, Abigail had weaved her web around Mr. Montgomery, giving her a head start. Even so, she wasn't taking any chances.

Gripping the reins tightly, Annie rode Phantom past the stalls. While she passed each one, Annie reached down to unlatch the doors. She then waved her cap in the air.

"Scat! Get out of here!" she hollered, stampeding the horses into the paddock.

* * *

On the outskirts of London, Annie felt the saddle inch slightly to one side. Should have cinched it tighter, she thought as she hunkered low. When Phantom got a sudden burst of speed, Annie couldn't hold on any longer and found herself sailing through the air.

Just before she hit the ground Annie tucked her head under at the last second. She rolled until she came to an sudden stop in a briar bush. Her hands trembled as she felt for broken bones. Satisfied that her injuries were minor—scrapes and bruises, she looked around for Phantom. To her dismay, she saw him galloping off in the direction of Spencer Estate.

Annie wasted no time running in the moonlight before she caught her foot in a rabbit hole. She heard a popping sound as she collapsed to the ground in pain. Gingerly touching her ankle, she realized it had ballooned to twice its normal size.

Impossible to walk, let alone run, Annie crawled. Even then, the pain was agonizing as she dragged her foot behind her.

She crawled until her knees were rubbed raw. Bits of gravel adhered to her bloodied skin.When she stumbled onto a broken tree limb, she pushed herself up to use it as a crutch. Annie gritted her teeth as she placed her injured foot on the dirt. "That bloody hurts!"

CHAPTER FIFTY-THREE

With the help of her makeshift crutch, Annie stumbled through London. Nearing the docks, she saw sailors celebrating their last night in England. As she passed the Black Anchor Pub, she collided with a sailor staggering out of the tavern.

"Watch where yer goin'."

The stocky sailor squished Annie's face between his broad hands. "Well, I'll be. I 'aven't seen ye in a long time. Thought the little maggot died or somethin'."

Annie's blood ran cold as she stared into Symington's eyes.

He mussed up her hair sending shivers down her spine. "Where's yer 'at?"

Symington then looked up and down the street. "Is Mr. Montgomery 'iding somewhere?" he muttered.

The smell of whiskey and rotting teeth turned Annie's stomach. "No, Symington, I'm alone." The words spilled out before the ramification of what she said hit her.

"Alone, are ye?" Like an animal stalking its prey, Symington eyed the stick. "Did ye 'urt yerself?"

"No." Annie stood straighter without putting more weight on the painful foot.

"Ye lie! Ye did 'urt yerself!"

Without warning, Symington kicked the stick out from under her. Fear emitted from every pore as Annie tumbled sideways.

"Why didn't ye tell me ye were 'urt?" he said. He bent down yanking a thistle out of her hair. "Let me take a look at yer leg."

Annie rubbed her scalp where a handful of hair, along with the thistle, was now missing. "I hurt my ankle."

Symington ran his calloused hands around both her ankles. "This one is swollen bad. Doc will need to take look at it. Ye think the cap'n will reward me?"

"Reward you for what?"

Symington let out a hearty laugh. "For bringing ye back to the ship. Bet 'e doesn't know yer 'ere, all by yer lonesome, now does 'e?"

If it means getting back to the Realm, I will promise him anything, she said to herself. "The captain will give you a reward, Symington, a big one," she said spreading her hands far apart.

"Me lucky day! One more dart game, and then I will take ye back to the ship. Now, don't go running off, Andrés," he said chuckling.

"Symington! Don't leave me here!"

"Don't want ye getting any ideas," he said as he picked up her walking stick and hurled it through the air. The sound of breaking glass dashed any hope of her making it back on her own.

Listening to his mocking laugh, Annie watched Symington stagger back to the Black Anchor Pub.

While her ankle throbbed, she looked around hoping to find someone else she knew, someone who would actually help and not abandon her. Her spirits lifted when a figure approached from the shadows.

"Andrés? Is that you?"

Annie could make out only his broad shoulders and long hair. The voice jolted her, though. It was familiar, but definitely not Barrette.

"Do I frighten you?"

"Should I be?" she asked.

He continued coming closer, his steps confident. He bent down and struck a match in her face. "If I hadn't heard that old sot call you by name, I might not have realized it was you."

For the first time, Annie wished Symington had stuck to calling her little maggot and not Andrés.

"The bigger question is do you remember me?" He hissed.

Annie's voice shook. "Lawrence?"

"So, you do remember me. I am flattered."

Annie sucked in her breath. "You can't still be angry that Captain Hawke chose me instead of you as his cabin boy."

"Are you forgetting? He did choose me. No matter, I was hired later that same day on another ship." He paused. "The Margaret Louise."

"You couldn't have been on the Margaret Louise. She sank. David Palmer was the only survivor."

"The captain's son survived? What a pity. Never liked him much."

Lawrence lit another match. He read Annie's expression well. "A bosun mate died on the Crimson Revenge before they seized the Margaret Louise. His misfortune was my good fortune. I replaced him.

"Would you like to know what I learned from Godenot and his crew?"

Annie kept quiet wondering how long Symington's dart game would be.

"I learned all about torture and revenge." Lawrence paused. "I wager Captain Hawke would be mighty sad if anything happened to his cabin boy. What do you think?"

Annie shouted as loud as she could, "Symington!"

Lawrence pulled out a knife, admiring its sharp blade in the moonlight. "Save your breath," he said. "Symington has forgotten you by now. This time I will gut you like a fish and no one will come to your rescue, not the captain, not anyone."

Lawrence parted Annie's bangs with his knife, nicking her forehead. A thin line of blood bubbled to the surface. "Taking your time when you are torturing someone can be a delightful experience."

Annie didn't flinch.

"My, my, aren't you the brave one."

"I have friends, Lawrence. You won't get away with this."

Lawrence stood up. He shouted to a group of sailors singing and staggering along the cobblestone street. "Are any of you Andrés' friends?"

Not a one even looked in their direction.

Out of the corner of her eye, though, Annie caught a glimmer of hope, a knife that dwarfed Lawrence's blade.

"Yer not being nice to me cap'n's cabin boy, now are ye?" Symington's voice boomed.

Startled, Lawrence quickly grabbed Annie. Clutching her like a human shield, Lawrence glared at Symington. "Take one more step closer, and I will slit the boy's throat."

Annie stopped digging her fingernails into Lawrence's flesh and held her breath.

"Drop your knife...now!" said yet another voice.

It came from behind Lawrence. Annie immediately recognized it—Barrette.

"Shoot me and you just might shoot Andrés, as well," Lawrence warned. "Are you willing to take that chance?"

Annie could feel Lawrence's rapid heartbeat. Trying to remain calm, Annie said, "He has a point, Barrette."

"Guess I'll have to take that chance!" Barrette shouted. "Drop the knife."

As the seconds ticked by, Annie hoped she wouldn't become one of Symington's stories told in the fo'c'sle.

Lawrence yielded.

"I wasn't going to hurt him," he muttered. "I just wanted to scare him."

Unwilling to risk his shipmate's life, Barrette struck Lawrence over the head.

The blow to his head sent Lawrence toppling forward. His knife remained at Annie's throat. As she fell along with Lawrence, she questioned Barrette's strategy.

CHAPTER FIFTY-FOUR

Symington wrenched Lawrence's arm away from Annie. Before she could reach for her throat to check for wounds, Barrette swooped down and caught her around her torso. She wasn't certain her ribs would survive his crushing hold.

"Careful with the little maggot," Symington said, "Don't want to bring back damaged goods to the Cap'n."

Barrette laid Annie down. "Are you all right?"

"I am now," she said. "When did you buy a pistol?"

"I didn't."

"If it's not yours, then whose is it?"

"I never had a pistol," Barrette said. "I picked up a rock and shoved it into Lawrence's back. Everything was happening so fast, I didn't know what else to do."

"So, I was saved by a rock?"

"No." He smiled. "You were saved by me."

Annie smiled back until she saw Symington tug up on Lawrence's thatch of blond hair with one hand, his knife in the other. "What are you doing?"

"Best I kill the mad dog," he said.

"Wait!" Annie shouted.

"Why?"

"If I hadn't caused that ruckus on the wharf months

ago, Lawrence would have been Captain Hawke's cabin boy and none of this would have happened."

"That don't change nothing. 'E still tried to kill ye."

"Look who's here," Annie heard Barrette say. "We do all the work and now Andrés' nursemaid shows up."

Mr. Montgomery reined in his horse. "When I saw Phantom along the road, I knew you couldn't have gotten far," he said to Annie as he slid off the saddle, tossing his reins to Barrette.

Annie looked up sheepishly. "Phantom threw me."

"I figured as much. You're lucky you didn't break your fool neck. Anything else you would like to tell me." Mr. Montgomery cocked his head. "Like who is that?"

"Lawrence," Annie said. "He attacked me…again.

Mr. Montgomery studied the unconscious youth's features. "Should I know this chap?"

"Lawrence is the fellow you dragged off the wharf before we sailed to the colonies. He is now one of Godenot´s men, a pirate."

"If he is a pirate, then why is he here?" Mr. Montgomery said.

"All I know is if it wasn't for Symington and Barrette, he would have killed me," Annie said.

"Get on your feet and I will take you back to the ship. Doc needs to look you over before I take you back to the Spencer's."

"The lad can't walk, sir," Symington said with slurred speech. "I think 'e broke 'is ankle."

Mr. Montgomery grabbed the reins from Barrette. He put his foot into the stirrup and swung himself into the saddle. "Hand...the boy to me. You two bring Lawrence back to the ship alive," he ordered.

Annie saw the disappointment on Symington's face as he picked her up and heaved her behind the cantle. "Remember, Mr. Montgomery, I saved the little maggot's life," he said.

"Symington, how many times must I tell you, his name is...?" Mr. Montgomery stopped. "I will put in a good word for you to the captain."

As he loosened the reins, he eyed Annie behind him. "You, young lady, have a lot of explaining to do," Mr. Montgomery said. "Hold on tight!"

Watching Annie clasp her arms firmly around the first mate's waist, Symington scratched his head. "Did I 'ear Mr. Montgomery call Andrés a 'lady?'"

Barrette howled with laughter. "That he did, Symington. That he did!"

CHAPTER FIFTY-FIVE

When Mr. Montgomery barged into Captain Hawke's cabin, he was greeted by blazing candlelight. Candles were everywhere, tall ones, short ones. Light danced on the overhead while shadows swayed.

"Doesn't anyone knock anymore?" Captain Hawke said from his chair.

"Are you trying to burn down our ship?"

"No, I was entertaining."

Mr. Montgomery sniffed a trace of perfume in the air before he spied two empty wine glasses on the table. He whispered, "Where is she?"

"The young woman departed rather abruptly, said I wasn't good company this evening." The captain took a swig from the bottle of port he clutched in his hand. "Were you able to cheer Annie up after I left?"

"Not exactly. Would you care to know what your cabin boy has been up to?"

"I no longer have a cabin boy. Remember?" He guzzled down the rest of the port.

"Well, Annie believes she is still your cabin boy. In fact, she was returning to the ship to prove it to you."

Captain Hawke tossed the empty bottle on the rug. "What are you talking about?"

"It is a long story."

"I have all the time in the world. Start from the beginning."

While they blew out the array of glowing candles, Mr. Montgomery briefed Captain Hawke on the evening's events: the letter to Abigail, the stampeded horses, Annie being thrown from Lord Spencer's horse, and her trek into London on her injured ankle.

"Didn't I tell you that cabin boys were too much trouble?" the captain said between puffs.

Mr. Montgomery licked his fingers to extinguish a flame. "I have saved the best for last, Jonathan. One of Godenot's men tried to kill her."

The captain turned so fast his sleeve nearly caught on fire from the one remaining candle. "A pirate tried to kill my cabin boy?"

"I thought you said you didn't have a cabin boy."

He ignored Mr. Montgomery's comment. "How badly is she hurt?" Captain Hawke asked.

"Don't look so worried, Jonathan. She was hurt worse from her fall from Lord Spencer's horse than from her encounter with Lawrence. She's with Doc, now."

"Lawrence? Who's Lawrence?" Captain Hawke said as he paced the floor.

"Lawrence is both the pirate and the fellow you picked to be your cabin boy before you chose Annie."

The captain shook his head and laughed.

"What's so amusing, Jonathan?"

"Not amusing, Matthew, ironic. I remember Annie saying how you have to look out for those quiet ones.

She was referring to Lawrence." Captain Hawke looked off into space. "Where is he now? Dead I hope."

"I told Barrette and Symington to bring him back to the ship...alive."

"Barrette and Symington?"

"Aye, they saved Annie's life."

"I want to question Symington and Barrette about Lawrence as soon as they are back on board."

"What about Annie?" Mr. Montgomery asked.

"Nothing has changed."

CHAPTER FIFTY-SIX

Mr. Montgomery informed Captain Hawke when Barrette and Symington returned to the Realm. When the captain found them in the fo'c'sle, both hopped to attention.

The captain thrust out his hand. "I believe thanks are in order."

Symington quickly wiped his hand across his shirt before shaking the captain's hand. "I was 'oping ye might cross me palm with a coin or two, Cap'n. Mind ye, I am not greedy, but I did save yer, uh, cabin girl's life. Barrette and me thinks Mr. Montgomery called 'im a lady."

"Aye, you heard right. My cabin boy is a girl." Looking at Symington's outstretched hand, he said, "Mr. Montgomery will compensate you both."

"I don't want a reward, Captain." Barrette said as the captain shook his hand.

"Can I 'ave 'is share?" Symington asked.

Captain Hawke nodded. "You can have his share, Symington, but right now, I want you to tell me everything you know about Lawrence and why he is here and not the Crimson Revenge?"

"He wasn't real talkative, Captain," Barrette said. "But he did tell us that the Crimson Revenge went aground during a storm. It broke up off the coast of France. Few survived. Godenot wasn't one of them,"

Captain Hawke thought a moment before ordering Barrette to stand guard outside Doc's quarters until Annie was safely off the ship.

"I'll look after her, Captain. You needn't worry. No harm will come to her on my watch," Barrette said.

The captain then turned to Symington. "Stand guard over Lawrence."

"We tied 'im up, Cap'n. That bloody pirate is going nowhere."

"I am sure you secured him good, Symington, but I don't want to take any chances of him getting loose."

Symington punched his fist into his hand. "It will be a pleasure, Cap'n."

"He will be turned over to the authorities." Captain Hawke muttered under his breath, "Pirates hang."

CHAPTER FIFTY-SEVEN

Annie grimaced in pain while Doc bound her ankle. When the door flew open, she forgot her discomfort. For a brief moment, Annie saw Barrette standing outside the door. But it was Captain Hawke, his jaw taut, that quickly changed her focus.

She imagined what a sight she must be. The knees of her trousers were completely gone, and the left sleeve ripped below her shoulder. She ran her hand through her hair, only to prick her finger on a spiky thistle. Annie peered into the captain's brooding eyes. Worry, relief? No, she thought, anger.

Captain Hawke studied Annie's toes peeking out from the bandage wrapped around her foot and ankle. "How bad is it, Doc?"

"Cuts, bruises, nothing serious. Her ankle might be broken, but it is so swollen, I can't be certain," Doc answered.

The captain stared at Annie. "I wish to talk to her alone, Doc."

"Certainly, Jonathan, but remember she has had a difficult time."

"And whose fault is that?"

Ah, thought Annie, there goes that eyebrow. And if there had been concern in the captain's voice before, it was now gone.

Looking like he had aged ten years in one night, Doc shuffled past Captain Hawke to the passageway. Annie braced herself for the onslaught she knew would soon follow. She didn't have long to wait.

A vein pulsated in the captain's neck, looking like it would burst at any moment. "How could you have done this to Doc? You are like a daughter to him. He left you safe at Spencer Manor looking like a fine young lady. Now look at you. And the Spencer's, they have done so much for you. You showed total disregard for everyone who cares about you."

Annie looked down at her hands. "I did not want to hurt anyone. I just thought…"

"What did you think, Annie? Or did you think at all?"

Annie's lips quivered. "I thought you needed a cabin boy. I thought you needed me to read to you."

The captain bristled. "Let me make this perfectly clear. I never wanted a cabin boy. It is Mr. Montgomery who insists I have one—him and his blasted traditions. But never again, I tell you, will I ever have another cabin boy."

He pulled out a steel case from his pocket, opening it to reveal a pair of Edward Scarlet spectacles. "I bought these after we docked in London. Ugly things, I know, but I can now read again." He lowered his voice. "I don't need you anymore, Annie."

His words pierced her heart like a sword. "I will leave, Captain, if that is what you want."

"That is what I want. At this very moment, Mr. Montgomery is on his way to the Spencers to let them know that you are safe and to make arrangements for your return to Spencer Estate."

He was almost to the door when Annie asked, "What will become of Lawrence?"

With his back to her, he said, "Pirates hang."

"Captain, I don't want him to hang."

He whirled around. "He's a bloody pirate. He tried to kill you!"

"None of this would have happened if Lawrence had been your cabin boy instead of me."

His eyes narrowed. "If he had been my cabin boy, I probably would have shot him by now."

"Lawrence told Barrette he was only trying to frighten me. I believe him. See." Annie raised her chin.

"What am I supposed to be looking at?"

"The mark on my neck," Annie said.

"Confounded things," Captain Hawke said as he fumbled to put his spectacles on. "I still don't see a mark."

"You don't see a mark, because there isn't one. I believe Lawrence pressed the back of his knife against my throat instead of the blade."

"That makes no sense."

"If he only intended to scare me, it makes sense. He cut my forehead using little pressure, so I know how sharp his knife was."

She felt the captain's warm breath on her neck as he examined her throat one last time.

"If he hadn't pressed the sharp side to your neck, then that only convinces me that Lawrence is simply stupid. Besides, it would have taken Lawrence no time to have turned the blade to your throat.

"All I know for certain is that he is a pirate, and pirates hang!"

"You didn't."

"I didn't what...hang?" Captain Hawke glared at her. "I was a pirate not by choice."

"Neither did Lawrence choose to be a pirate. He was taken off the Margaret Louise."

"But he embraced it. I didn't"

"Please, Captain, I do not want Lawrence to hang."

"When he is turned in to the proper authorities, it will be out of my hands."

"Surely, Mr. Montgomery must know someone in high places who can get him a pardon," Annie said.

With his back to her, Captain Hawke hesitated in the doorway. Annie expected him to say something, but he was silent. As the door closed, Annie knew her life as a sailor had ended.

CHAPTER FIFTY-EIGHT

Captain Hawke headed for the cargo hold where Lawrence was lashed to a barrel. Dried blood matted the young man's hair, a deep gash across his cheek. His right eye was swollen shut, his lips puffy and purple. Fresh blood dripped from the corner of his mouth.

The captain knew Symington had been keeping more than a watchful eye on the Realm's notorious guest.

"Untie him."

"Aye, Aye, Cap'n." Symington unfastened the ropes across the young pirate's chest.

"Stand up ye mad dog! Show the cap'n some respect!" Symington said. For added encouragement, he kicked Lawrence.

The young pirate's face contorted in pain, but he made no attempt to stand.

"You are dismissed, Symington," Captain Hawke said.

"After the cap'n gets through with ye, ye'll wish I'd put ye out of yer misery! No one 'urts the cap'n's cabin boy and gets away with it!" Symington said as he sauntered off.

Lawrence rubbed his hands together. "Get on with it!"

"I want to know what happened to Godenot," Captain Hawke said.

Lawrence didn't say a word.

The captain knelt down looking into Lawrence's cold blue eyes. "I want to know what happened to Godenot."

"I told your two men already and look what that old sailor did to me."

"If I had my way, I would do far worse, but Annie doesn't want you harmed."

"Annie? Who is Annie?"

A satisfied smirk spread across the captain's face. "Oh, I forgot. You know her by another name... Andrés."

"You lie!"

"My cabin boy is a girl and *she* wants your life spared." Captain Hawke sneered.

Lawrence smiled. "I always did have a way with the ladies."

The captain seized Lawrence's throat. "If it was up to me, I would rip you limb from limb with my bare hands!"

Reluctantly, he withdrew his hand.

Lawrence clutched his throat, gasping for air. "Drowned. Godenot drowned just like I told them."

Not convinced, the captain asked, "You *saw* him drown?"

Pain wrinkled Lawrence's brow. "I didn't see him drown, but you know what Godenot looked like. If he had made it to shore, I would have seen him."

SECRETS OF THE REALM

Captain Hawke remembered Godenot all too well, a giant of a man with white hair down to his waist and merciless dark eyes. "Aye, he would be hard to miss."

CHAPTER FIFTY-NINE

Annie felt uncomfortable wearing the powder-blue dress Mr. Montgomery had brought back from Spencer Estate. Captain Hawke made it clear that she would leave the ship as Annie Moore and not Andrés de la Cruz.

Looking over her shoulder, Annie gazed at the Realm's crew crowding the rail of the anchored ship. With his mop of tight red curls, Samuel Baggott was easy to pick out. Mr. Allan stood next to Mr. Waverly. It was the first time Annie had seen the cook out of the galley.

Annie looked at Ainsworth and Smitty rowing her and Doc to the wharf. They, too, were quiet. They didn't look at her. They looked through her.

Andrés no longer existed and neither did Annie. She was a stranger to them all. The sailors had lost one of their shipmates, but this one wouldn't be buried out at sea.

"What will become of Andrés?" Annie whispered to Doc.

"What do you mean, Annie?"

"Will they remember him…remember me. Will we become characters in one of Symington's tall tales or simply forgotten?"

Doc patted her knee. "I assure you, Annie, you will not be forgotten."

Once on the wharf, Mr. Montgomery carried Annie to her sea chest. After setting her down, he kneaded her right shoulder, the only spot that wasn't sore. He then walked off leaving Annie and Doc to await Lord Spencer's carriage.

When she heard the high-stepping horses prance onto the wharf, Annie thought her spirits couldn't sink any lower.

Robert swung open the carriage door for Lord Spencer and Abigail. Annie watched Captain Hawke greet them. He took Lord Spencer aside, engaging him in conversation.

Seeing Abigail giggle, Annie wondered how her friend's conversation with Mr. Montgomery could possibly be of a lighthearted nature after everything Annie had been through. When Abigail looked at Annie, her smile faded. She let go of Mr. Montgomery's hand and walked toward Annie.

She examined Annie's bandaged ankle and the large bruise that had blossomed on her cheek. "Are you in pain?"

Annie was grateful that Abigail's voice didn't sound condemning.

"I'm not in much pain," Annie said.

Doc added. "Her ankle is too swollen to tell if it is broken or just a bad sprain. Either way, she must stay off it for at least six weeks."

Mr. Montgomery walked up to Annie. "It is time to

go," he said. He then scooped Annie up into his arms and waited for Symington and Barrette to say their goodbyes.

"Stay out of trouble ye little…princess," Symington said while he flipped a gold coin into the air. "Me reward from the cap'n."

After he pocketed the coin, Annie said to him. "You earned it, Symington"

The old sea dog winked at her before ambling off to the boat.

Annie leaned her head on Mr. Montgomery's shoulder while Barrette brushed her bangs out of her eyes. "I always knew there was something special about you," he said. "Even with that bruise on your cheek, you are a pretty one."

Not prepared for Barrette's gentle touch or his soothing voice, Annie blushed. I could get lost in those dimples of his, she said to herself.

He kissed her on the cheek ever so gently, but Captain Hawke didn't let Annie savor the moment.

"To the boat, Barrette." He snarled.

The captain's raised eyebrow didn't shock her as much as his flared nostrils. Why was he so angry with Barrette, she wondered.

CHAPTER SIXTY

While Robert hauled the sea chest to the carriage, Mr. Montgomery sat Annie on the red upholstered seat. "Captain Hawke wanted you to know that everything has been arranged."

"I assume you mean Lawrence won't hang?"

"Unfortunately, that is a correct assumption." Mr. Montgomery slid his hand into his pocket and took out her cap. "I thought you might want this, a keepsake, perhaps. I found it caught on a branch near the stable."

"Why would I want that ugly thing?"

"If that is how you feel, I will dispose of it."

Mr. Montgomery was about to jettison the Monmouth cap off the wharf when Annie called out. "No, wait! Maybe, my cousin will want it."

"Erik will be most pleased," Mr. Montgomery said with a quick smile.

* * *

While the carriage bounced along the cobblestone road, Abigail told Annie of her plans. "Father has arranged to have your bedroom in the west wing. It overlooks the rose garden. I will have the one next to it. Won't that be splendid?"

Annie wasn't interested in bedrooms or rose gardens. She saw nothing splendid about anything.

As the fog rolled in, Annie drew the silk curtain over the window. Her other hand touched the cap lying next to her. The cap wasn't ugly, not really, she thought. It was like an old friend, one who would remind her each day of the Realm and her crew.

"Annie, have you gone deaf?" Lord Spencer said. "That is the second time I have called your name, child. Here."

He handed Annie a letter sealed with an embossed red hawk on it.

"What is this?" she asked.

"It is from the captain."

Annie took the letter and swallowed hard.

"Open it." Abigail urged, her eyes wide with anticipation.

"Hasn't he said enough cruel things to me? Must I now read them in a letter?"

"If you won't open it, I will." Abigail said.

Annie batted her hand away. "It is *my* letter and I shall do what I want with it."

She broke the waxed seal. The strokes of the letters were bold with nary a slant nor fancy embellishments, much like the captain himself, she thought.

"I must hear every word." Abigail said.

Annie began, "*My dearest Annie…*"

"Dearest," Abigail gushed. "The captain sounds quite taken with you."

"Abigail, 'dearest' is an appropriate salutation to a young woman. Please, Annie, continue. And you, daughter, quiet." Lord Spencer said.

"I shall never hire another cabin boy again..." Annie stopped. "See, all he wants to do is humiliate me."

Her first instinct was to crumple up the letter, and toss it out of the carriage. Instead, she folded it carefully and put it back in the envelope. She then handed it to Lord Spencer.

"If you don't want to read it, why can't I?" Abigail said as she unsuccessfully tried to intercept it. "It can't be all bad."

Lord Spencer took the letter. "Perhaps, you will want to read the letter another time, Annie."

"You can burn it as far as I'm concerned."

CHAPTER SIXTY-ONE

Five weeks after the Realm left her moorings, Annie languished at Spencer Manor. Each day, chambermaid Molly had the unenviable job of bringing Annie her meals. When the girl came to retrieve the dishes, Annie often hurled food or dishes at her, sometimes both. The final insult came when Annie, propped up on her fluffy pillows, watched Molly clean up the mess.

Since Molly never complained, and she knew when to duck, the daily spectacle was losing its appeal for Annie. Sitting in her canopy bed, Annie spotted the maid peering cautiously around the door jamb.

"You can come in," Annie said.

Her tray sat on the bed, the food barely touched.

"I promise not to throw anything at you."

Looking at the tray, Molly's smile turned into a frown. "You must eat milady. You are wastin' away."

"I do not care if I waste away, and I am no lady." Neither am I a sailor, Annie thought to herself.

"I want to be called Annie, not milady." Feeling generous, she added, "Please."

Molly's bright smile returned. "It is day time, Miss Annie. You should have sunlight, not candlelight in here. Let me open the curtains for you. And if you like,

I can help you to the window."

Annie rolled a pear in her hand. "Touch those curtains, Molly, and I might have to throw this at you after all."

Standing in the doorway, Abigail broke up Annie's pity party. "Molly you can go now."

The chambermaid gathered up Annie's tray of dishes and hurried off.

"Today, you are going to the garden. The fresh air will do you good," Abigail said.

Annie slouched under the covers. "I didn't want to go to the garden yesterday or the day before that. So why do you think today will be any different?"

"I really don't care what you want anymore. I understand you miss your friends on the Realm, but I can't do anything about that."

"They are called shipmates, not friends."

"Friends, shipmates, what difference does it make? Apparently, you have forgotten that I was once your friend. All I am asking is for you to come to the garden with me."

"No offense, Abigail, but I can't walk. Remember? I broke my ankle."

"Erik will carry you."

"I do not want him carrying me anywhere."

"It has already been arranged. By the way, Matthew will be visiting today and you will be on your best behavior. Is that understood?"

Annie had not seen Mr. Montgomery since the Realm set sail. As angry as she was with Captain

Hawke, she was even angrier with Mr. Montgomery for his transgression, abandoning the captain for Abigail. Annie would have gladly taken his place on the Realm if given the chance. Is there no honor, she wondered.

When her cousin came into the room, Annie glowered at Abigail. "I see you are serious about me not having any choice in the matter." She pulled out a pillow from behind her back and heaved it at Erik.

He caught it with one hand. "Missed," he said and heaved it back at her, nailing her in the face. She fired more pillows at him until she ran out of ammunition.

"It is indeed a lovely day. The birds are chirping, flowers blooming." He grinned broadly at the pillows scattered across the room.

His forced cheerfulness grated on Annie's nerves. "I do not want to ever see the light of day again." She dug her fingers into the comforter.

He continued to smile. "If I have to, I will throw you over my shoulder like a sack of potatoes. Or maybe you can act like a lady…"

"I am not a lady!" Annie screamed at him.

"As I was saying, maybe you can *act* like a lady and let me carry you to the garden. Which is it, Annie, sack of potatoes or lady? Your choice."

"Well, I'll be, I'm actually being given a choice about something?"

Coming along the side of the bed, Erik lost his cheerfulness. "Raise your arms—now."

Too weary to argue, Annie made a request. "I

cannot go outside in my bedclothes. I would like to change first."

"Here, take this." Abigail grabbed a shawl hanging over a chair and handed it to Annie. "I do not want you changing your mind."

Annie wrapped the shawl around her shoulders and allowed Erik to carry her. She buried her nose in his shoulder. She smelled the scent of the horses from the stable.

Once in the garden, Erik placed Annie on one of two oak benches. She closed her eyes and welcomed the breeze brushing against her cheeks. It reminded her of climbing the ratlines with Christopher. A lifetime ago, she thought.

"I brought you a book, Annie, one of your favorites," Abigail said. "Shakespeare sonnets."

Annie opened her eyes. She took the book, skimmed its pages, and placed it next to her.

She looked off into the distance and saw Mr. Montgomery strolling toward them. He wore a narrow-sleeved pastel blue waistcoat, tan breeches and black riding boots. As hard as she tried, Annie could not help but be amused that Mr. Montgomery's coat was a perfect match to the color of Abigail's dress. She wondered if they were now consulting each other on what to wear. Annie wrapped the shawl tighter around her body.

Behind Mr. Montgomery followed Robert and another footman. Annie saw that they were carrying a large wooden box. She guessed it was about forty inches long by twenty inches wide. The closer they got, the straighter Annie sat up.

They placed the chest, with its brass handles and dovetailed corners, at Annie's feet. She bent down; tracing the letters of the name carved on the front, Christopher. She breathed in the familiar aroma of the Realm. Her lips twitched up at the corners of her mouth. The smile disappeared as quickly as it had appeared.

"Why did you bring this here, to torment me?" Annie protested.

"We thought it was time you..." Abigail struggled to find the right words.

Mr. Montgomery came to her rescue. "We thought it was time you moved on."

"What does this have to do with my moving on?" Annie said while she pointed to the chest.

"I believe what is inside the chest will bring you some comfort," he said.

Annie lowered her voice. "All that is inside are my clothes and a few trinkets, like the knife that Captain Hawke gave me. And since I hold only contempt for that man, I cannot imagine how this can bring me comfort."

"Annie, there is much more in there than you think," Abigail said. She opened the lid halfway before Annie slapped her hand on top of Abigail's.

"I will open it. After all, it is *my* sea chest," Annie said.

She slowly opened the lid and gazed at the monkey

knife lying on top of her clothes.

"A mighty fine lookin' knife, that is," Erik said, staring at the monkey's eyes. "What kind of gems are those?"

"Rubies. You can have the knife, Erik."

He couldn't stop staring at the ruby eyes. "Are you certain you want me to have it?"

The more she thought about it, no, she didn't want him to have it. Like the sea chest, it was another connection to the Realm. And while she wouldn't admit it to anyone, they were all still an important part of her life.

Annie wouldn't go back on her word, though, and handed him the belt with the sheathed weapon. "Promise me you will take good care of it."

"I promise."

She watched him strain to put on the belt. It barely went halfway around his waist.

Annie shrugged. "I'm sorry, Erik, but you cannot have the knife without the belt."

Erik smacked his thigh and chuckled. "You had no intention of givin' it to me. Did you?"

"Forgive me, but the more I thought about it, I just couldn't."

"I understand. Now let's see what else is in this here chest that I can't have."

Annie watched Erik rummage through her things. She felt a knot growing in her throat as each item came into view: her fearnought jacket, shirt, canvas trousers, and the gray socks. Then she glimpsed something shiny. "What is that?"

She pushed herself off the bench to get a closer look. Careful not to put weight on her broken ankle, Annie knelt down. She uncovered a mirror and brush.

Annie looked at Mr. Montgomery. "This belonged to Emily, Doc's wife. And what is this? I never put these things in here," she exclaimed.

"Doc wanted you to have the brush and mirror, Annie," Mr. Montgomery said. "The other items are from the rest of the crew."

"I don't understand. Why would they do that?"

"Because they care about you, Annie," Abigail said. "We all care about you."

"Except for Barrette and Symington, no one would even look me in the eye. They treated me like a stranger."

"They were trying to get used to the fact that Andrés never existed," Mr. Montgomery said. "But Baggott told me he wanted to put one of his favorite possessions, a deck of cards, in your sea chest. He hoped you would remember him and the Realm. The idea caught on. Even if they couldn't put it into words, the crew wanted you to know how much you meant to them."

Annie found one keepsake after another in the sea chest, a star knot from Mr. Allan, Smitty's whalebone carving. She held up a nail and laughed. "This must be from Symington."

"Aye," Mr. Montgomery said.

She blushed when she pulled out Barrette's white

linen shirt.

Annie resumed searching through the chest. "Oh my."

"What is it?" Abigail said as she knelt beside Annie. "Another shirt?"

Annie rolled her eyes at Abigail. "No, it is a book of poetry by Thomas Dekker. There is a poem in here that the captain and I both love, *Old Fortunatus*."

"Captain Hawke wanted you to have this," Mr. Montgomery said as he handed her an object wrapped in plain paper.

Annie had noticed it earlier, but when her attention focused on the sea chest, she forgot about what Mr. Montgomery was holding. She hesitated, but her curiosity won out. She took it in both hands and shook it. She then felt its corners. She knew what it had to be.

"Open it." Abigail insisted.

Annie ripped off the paper. Her eyes widened. "I can't believe it."

Erik couldn't hide his disappointment. "Not another book."

Annie scanned the pages. "Not just any book, Erik. It is a book of poetry by Garcilaso de la Vega. Me mum used to read it to me when I was a child. I told the captain about it on my first day on the Realm." Annie turned to Mr. Montgomery. "Where did he get it?"

"In Charles Town," Mr. Montgomery said. "Jonathan searched for a copy of the book. He was about to give up when he discovered that Captain Delgado had a copy. He offered to purchase it from him. Eduardo would accept no amount of money since it was a gift for his wife. But Jonathan thought he might be able to tempt Eduardo with one of his prized weapons. I won't bore you with the details."

"But it wasn't one of his knives, was it?"

Mr. Montgomery cocked his head. "You know?"

"It was the sword he displayed among his knives. It was beautiful with its chiseled acanthus design. When I saw it was missing, I asked him about it. He said he lost it in a card game. I don't understand. If he wanted me have it, then why didn't he just give it to me," Annie said.

"He had his reasons," Mr. Montgomery said.

"And now, I can't even thank him," Annie said.

"Oh, don't worry your pretty little head about that," Abigail said. "We have saved the best for last. Haven't we, Matthew."

Mr. Montgomery nodded his head.

Lord Spencer, who had been listening quietly under a large oak tree, walked across the lawn. He reached into his coat, and pulled out an envelope. "Do you remember this?"

Annie immediately recognized the broken waxed seal of a red hawk on the envelope. "It is Captain Hawke's letter, the one you gave me in the carriage."

"You told me I could burn it, but I always thought you should have it. I took the liberty of reading it. "

"You read *my* letter?"

"Yes, I did and now I know you must read it." He handed the letter to Annie.

She took a deep breath. "*My dearest Annie…*"

And like the first time Annie had begun reading the letter, Abigail gushed. "The captain sounds quite taken with you."

Annie ignored her and continued reading. "*I shall never hire another cabin boy again. Not because you were too much trouble, but because you can never be replaced.*"

She looked at Abigail. "I thought he hated me."

"You are so silly, Annie. How could anyone hate you?" Abigail said. "Now, continue with the letter."

"*When I return from China.*" Annie paused once more.

"Mr. Montgomery, the captain must have been quite angry with you when you told him you wouldn't be returning to the ship. The voyage to China was something you both had been planning ever since the Realm first sailed."

"I thought he would chastise me for leaving the Realm for a woman, but if anything, he seemed envious," Mr. Montgomery said.

"The captain is a wise man, Mathew. He knew you had better things to do than going to China," Abigail said as she tiptoed her fingers up Mr. Montgomery's arm.

Lord Spencer banged his cane on the bench. "Abigail!"

"Now, now, Father, you will get a case of apoplexy if you let yourself get all worked up." She turned to Annie. "Finish reading."

"*I wager my entire knife collection that your adventures*

will continue on dry land. You will surely keep the Spencer household jumping once your ankle has healed."

Annie thought a moment. "Do you suppose he would consider using a chambermaid for target practice as an adventure?"

Erik shook his head. "No, has to be something more exciting if you ask me."

"Don't give her any ideas," Abigail said.

Annie couldn't help but laugh. It felt good. She went back to reading the letter. *"When you long for the Realm, open your sea chest and know that we have not forgotten you. We never will.*

"Upon my return, you and I must swap tales of our adventures. But remember this, you are a fine young lady now, and your adventures will be far different from when you were out at sea."

Annie placed the letter on her lap and sighed. "That is all he wrote."

"How did he sign it?" Abigail asked.

"Captain Jonathan Hawke."

"That's all?" Abigail said.

"How else should he have signed it?" Annie asked.

Abigail put her finger to her temple. "How about this: Now that you are gone, my heart beats slower?"

"Daughter, it is not a love letter," Lord Spencer said shaking his head.

"What can I say, Father? I am a romantic."

While everyone discussed the letter, Annie quietly read it to herself, again. She memorized every word, every detail, before tenderly slipping it back into its envelope. Now that he is gone, it is my heart that beats slower, she thought to herself.

She pushed that thought aside. "Lord Spencer, may I borrow your cane?" she asked

Conversation came to a halt. All eyes fell on Annie.

"My cane?" Lord Spencer said.

"I need it for only a moment, sir. I will give it right back."

Lord Spencer handed it to her.

Leaning on the cane, Annie steadied herself and stood up. Both Erik and Abigail reached out, but she waved them off. "I am fine," she said. "In fact, I am better than fine."

"Huzzah!" Mr. Montgomery cheered, "I do believe we have our Annie back."

Dark clouds rolled in while thunder boomed in the distance. Mr. Montgomery took off his coat and held it over Abigail's head when the first drop fell.

Shielded from the pelting rain, Abigail said to Annie, "Have Erik carry you back." She and Mr. Montgomery rushed off.

Erik had already draped his coat over Annie's shoulders and was about to pick her up when she stopped him. "Please, Erik, not yet. The rain makes me feel like I am out at sea."

Annie tucked her damp hair behind each ear. "Once my ankle is completely healed, I shall begin my adventures."

"Your adventures will be far different on land than when you were out at sea," Erik said.

Annie shot him a sly grin. "Hmm, I wonder what sort of adventures are befitting a fine lady such as myself. Whatever they are, Captain Hawke will not be disappointed."

NO AR 2/3/20

CPSIA information can be obtained at www.ICGtesting.com
Printed in the USA
LVOW11s2009071014

407667LV00007B/1040/P